HANK ZIPZER

The World's Greatest Underachiever

NIAGARA FALLS, OR DOES IT?

by Henry Winkler and Lin Oliver

HANK ZIPZER

The World's Greatest Underachiever

NIAGARA FALLS, OR DOES IT?

Grosset & Dunlap • New York

Text copyright © 2003 by Fair Dinkum and Lin Oliver Productions, Inc. Illustrations copyright © 2003 by Grosset & Dunlap. All rights reserved. Published by Grosset & Dunlap, a division of Penguin Young Readers Group, 345 Hudson Street, New York, NY, 10014. GROSSET & DUNLAP is a trademark of Penguin Group (USA) Inc. Published simultaneously in Canada. Printed in the U.S.A.

Library of Congress Cataloging-in-Publication Data
Winkler, Henry, 1945-
Niagara Falls, or does it? / by Henry Winkler and Lin Oliver.
p. cm. — (Hank Zipzer, the mostly true confessions of the world's best underachiever)
Summary: Fourth-graders Hank, Ashley, and Frankie are excitedly preparing for a magic show at the Rock 'N Bowl when Hank's creative alternative to an English essay lands him in detention and grounded the week of the show.
[1. Schools—Fiction. 2. Magic tricks—Fiction. 3. Learning disabilities—Fiction. 4. Humorous stories.]   I. Oliver, Lin. II. Title.   III. Series.
PZ7.W72934Ni 2003
[Fic]—dc21   2003005962

ISBN 0-448-43162-9 (pbk)   F G H I J

ISBN 0-448-43232-3 (hc)   D E F G H I J

I dedicate this book to my wife Stacey and my three children, Jed, Zoe and Max, because it's their love that gave me the strength to do this in the first place—H.W.

This book is for my four fabulous men— Alan, Theo, Oliver and Cole. With love and potato leek soup—L.O.

CHAPTER 1

IT STARTED TO BUZZ. I looked up. The loud speaker above the door crackled and buzzed again. Then it started to shake. It was coming alive!

"Hank Zipzer!" the loudspeaker said. "Report to Principal Love's office at once."

I put my hands over my ears and slid down in my chair.

How did it know my name? It was only the first hour of the first day of school, and already my name was coming out of that box on the wall.

Everyone in class stared at me. Some kids giggled. A few of them whispered. But not Nick McKelty. Nope—he cupped his hands over his big mouth and shouted, "Way to go, Zipper Boy."

My teacher, Ms. Adolf, shot me a really nasty look.

Show no fear, I thought. Walk the walk.

I stood up and strutted to the door like Shaquille O'Neal taking center court. Okay, so I wear a size-four shoe and he wears a twenty-three—it's the attitude that counts. I'm long on attitude. Short on shoe but long on attitude.

When I reached the door, I turned to my best friend, Frankie Townsend. "If I don't come back," I told him, "you can have my protractor."

"Don't forget to breathe in there," Frankie whispered. "Remember, Zip, oxygen is power."

Frankie is very big on oxygen. Whenever I'm nervous, he always tells me to take some deep breaths. He learned that from his mom, who is a yoga teacher. She's really good at yoga. In fact, she's not good, she's great. She is so flexible, she can lift up her leg and put her foot in her pocket!

Even though I was going to the principal's office, I was determined to leave with style, my head held high. I flashed the class my best smile, the one where I show both my top and bottom teeth. Then, in the middle of maybe the greatest exit ever, the loudspeaker buzzed again.

"And don't you dare stop in the bathroom, young man," it said.

Now how did it know I was going to do that?

Everyone laughed as I left.

"No laughing in class!" Ms. Adolf shouted, banging on her desk with this pointer stick she has.

That's one of her rules. Ms. Adolf doesn't believe in laughing. She thinks fourth-graders laugh way too much.

There are two fourth-grade teachers in my school. One is named Mr. Sicilian, and he's really nice. He plays soccer with everyone at recess and never gives homework on the weekends. The other is Ms. Adolf. She doesn't play any games and gives two tons of homework even on weekends. My luck, I got Ms. Adolf.

I could practically hear my heart pounding as I walked down the hall. Principal Love has a way of making you nervous, especially when you don't know what you've done wrong.

I was trying not to think about him, so I

looked at all the "Welcome Back" decorations in the hall instead. The halls in my school are painted yuck green. You know, the color of melted pistachio ice cream. But the decorations really helped cheer things up. I liked Miss Hart's door, which had an underwater theme. All the fifth-graders in her class had pasted pictures of their faces onto octopus heads. Mr. Sicilian's was my favorite. All the kids' heads were soccer balls. I told you he was cool.

When I reached the stairs, I thought about sliding down the banister, but I was already in enough trouble, so I took the steps—two at a time. My mouth was dry when I got to the bottom, so I stopped at the water fountain to get a drink.

Just as I took the first swallow, the loud-speaker buzzed again.

"I'm waiting, Mr. Zipzer," it said. Principal Love has the kind of voice that sounds like it belongs to a really tall man with a lot of bushy, black hair. But actually, Principal Love is short and bald except for a little fringe of red hair.

I ran down the hall. I couldn't get in trouble for running in the halls if the place I was running to was the principal's office, right?

When I got to the office, I took a deep breath. I looked up at the sign above the door. LELAND LOVE, PRINCIPAL, it said. I had been here before. Many times. Too many times. Way, way, way too many times.

Slowly, I pushed open the door. I walked inside and came face to face with the five of them. No, not people—there was only one person there. I'm talking about *things*. The things on Principal Love's face: two eyes, two ears, and one mole on his cheek that looked like the Statue of Liberty without the torch. I don't know if it's possible for a mole to frown, but trust me, this one did not look happy.

"Approach me, young man," Principal Love said.

I wanted to, I really did, but my feet were stuck on his carpet. It was as if I had big wads of gum stuck to the soles of my shoes.

"Were you or were you not tardy today?" Principal Love asked.

I didn't answer because I've found that when Leland Love asks a question, he likes to answer it himself.

"You were seventeen minutes late," he said. See what I mean?

"Did we not have this talk thirty times in third grade, fifteen times in second grade, and I won't even refer to first grade?" Principal Love's face twitched. It looked like the Statue of Liberty was doing a hula dance.

I tried not to laugh. That would have gotten me into even bigger trouble.

"We've had this talk many times," he answered himself. See, he did it again.

I looked down at my feet, mostly to keep from staring at the Statue of Liberty mole. Once you focus on that thing, it's really hard to take your eyes off it. I noticed that I had put on two different socks again. One had a Nike swoosh, and the other was just your basic Wal-Mart sock.

"If there's one thing I want you to learn from your experience at PS 87, it is this." Principal Love was using his bushy-hair-tall-man voice. "Are you listening, young man?"

"I've got both ears working, sir."

Actually, I was listening. I really was curious to hear the single most important thing I was supposed to learn in my whole entire elementary school career.

Principal Love cleared his throat. "Always be on time, when time is involved," he said.

Wow. There it was. Now, if I could just figure out what it meant.

"Explain to me how it is possible that you were late on the very first day of school," he said.

Okay, I'll be honest with you. I am late a lot, but I don't mean to be. In fact, I try really hard to have everything ready on time—my pencils all sharpened; my three ballpoint pens ready to roll; a protractor, a ruler *and* a compass in my pencil case. But this morning I had a problem. I'm pretty sure I remember putting my backpack on my desk chair before I went to bed. But somehow, and I don't have an exact reason for this, my backpack played hide-and-seek during the night and this morning it took me twenty minutes to find it. It was in the coat closet by the front door. But try telling that to Leland Love.

"I'm waiting for an answer," said Principal Love.

And all that squeaked out of me was, "Can't explain it, sir."

"Well then, absorb this," he said, "because I'm only going to say it once. Punctuality and the fourth grade go hand in hand." He paused, then said it again, just like I knew he would. "Punctuality and the fourth grade go hand in hand."

I'm not sure but I think the Statue of Liberty on his face nodded in agreement.

CHAPTER 2

I CAN'T BELIEVE I'm saying this, but it was actually a relief to get back to Ms. Adolf's class . . . for about twenty seconds, anyway.

As soon as I slid into my chair, the words *"Five full paragraphs are required"* came flying out of Ms. Adolf's mouth like heat-seeking missiles.

I looked around. All the other kids were writing in their assignment books. I reached for my assignment book, too, but it was missing in action. I thought maybe I had left it in the middle drawer of my desk at home, underneath my broken watch collection. Or maybe on the kitchen table.

"The topic for your essay is: What I did on my summer vacation," Ms. Adolf went on. As she wrote the words on the blackboard, I noticed that her skirt had a bunch of chalk marks in the butt region. That happens to teachers when they lean against the blackboard, but I had never seen chalk marks like this before. They looked like donkey ears. When I thought of Ms. Adolf with a donkey on her butt, I couldn't help myself. I laughed out loud.

"Henry, I see nothing funny," Ms. Adolf said. Of course she didn't. That's because she couldn't see her rear end.

I bit my lip and tried to concentrate.

"I expect you to write an opening paragraph, a concluding paragraph, and three supporting paragraphs," Ms. Adolf was saying.

I raised my hand.

"Exactly how long does a paragraph have to be?" I asked.

Everyone laughed, which was strange, because I wasn't trying to be funny. Ms. Adolf didn't laugh. She got little red splotches on her neck, like the kind my sister, Emily, gets when she's really mad.

"Well, Henry," she said, saying my name as if it smelled bad. "We will all learn that from you, since you'll be the first one to read your composition out loud to the class."

Ms. Adolf walked to her desk. She wore a lanyard around her neck with a small key on it. The key was silver and so shiny that she must have polished it every night. She slipped the lanyard off and unlocked the top drawer of her desk with the key. I wondered what could be in there that had to be locked up. I looked at Frankie, who knew what I was thinking.

"Maybe she's got a big wad of cash in there," he whispered.

"Or jewels," said our friend Ashley Wong, who loves jewelry.

But when Ms. Adolf opened the drawer, the only thing she took out was her roll book. She picked it up and started to write.

"Henry Zipzer, Monday at nine-fifteen. We will all look forward to hearing your essay then. Is that clear, Henry?"

"Ms. Adolf," I said, "do you think you could call me Hank?"

"Why would I call you *Hank* when *Henry* is a perfectly fine name?" she said. She locked up her roll book and slipped the key back over her head.

"It's what my friends call me."

"Well, *I* am not your friend," Ms. Adolf said. As if I hadn't already figured that out.

She reached down and picked a tiny piece of lint off her skirt. I mean, it was so tiny you needed a microscope to see it. She held the shred of lint in her hand and walked it carefully over to the wastebasket. When she dropped it in, I'm telling you, I saw nothing leave her fingers.

I wondered why Ms. Adolf would care so much about a piece of lint. It's not like she looks that good anyway. All she ever wears is a gray skirt and a gray blouse, which match her gray hair and gray glasses, not to mention her gray face.

"Remember, class, that's five paragraphs," she said. "And neatness counts. I'll be expecting your very best work. That includes you, Henry."

Smile, Hank, I thought. Nod your head, up and down. You can do this. Five paragraphs. What's the big deal? You've got six days.

Oh come on, who am I kidding? I can't even write *one* good sentence. So how am I ever going to write an entire five-paragraph essay? Ms. Adolf might as well have asked me to ski down Mount Everest . . . backwards . . . blindfolded . . . and butt naked.

CHAPTER 3

AT LUNCH, I SAT at the table and stared at my vegetarian bologna sandwich. Most of the other kids were waiting in the hot food line. It was either macaroni-and-cheese day or tuna-melt day. Or maybe it was both. I couldn't tell without looking at the menu, because all the cafeteria food smells the same.

I looked around the lunchroom and spotted Frankie. He had just bought a milk and was laughing and talking with Katie Sperling and Kim Paulson, only the two most beautiful girls in the entire school. When Frankie smiles, he gets this huge dimple in his cheek. As he walked, he kept flashing the girls The Big Dimple. And, man, was it working! They were following him to our table. I couldn't believe it—Katie Sperling and Kim Paulson were going to sit down with us! That is, until Robert

Upchurch cut in front of them and took the seat across from me.

"Hey, Hank, mind if I sit here?" he asked.

"Yes," I answered, but it was too late.

When Katie and Kim saw Robert, they swerved left—at least I think it was left. Maybe it was right. It's hard for me to keep track of directions. Anyway, they went down a totally different aisle and sat down with Ryan Shimozato and his friends. Robert isn't exactly a girl magnet. He has a neck the size of a pencil and always wears a starchy white shirt with a tie. (That's right, I said a *tie*.) Add to that the fact that he's the most boring person on the planet, and you can't blame the girls for picking another table.

Frankie flopped down next to me. "Thanks, Robert," he said. "Nice work."

"What'd I do?" Robert asked. Poor kid, he really didn't have a clue.

Robert just started third grade. Since the third-graders and fourth-graders at my school eat lunch together, this was the first day he'd gotten a chance to sit with us. We don't really want him hanging around with us, but he lives in the same apartment building as Frankie, Ashley, and me, so he thinks he has the right to tag along everywhere.

Frankie glanced at my sandwich and made a face. He's been making faces at my lunches ever since we were in preschool.

"I see your mom's at it again," he said. "What's she calling this, soy surprise?"

"It's bologna," I told him.

"Bologna and I go *way* back," said Frankie. "And this is no bologna!"

I don't know if you've had vegetarian bologna before, but I don't think you've ever had my *mom's* vegetarian bologna. She thinks she invented it, which proves she should keep her thoughts to herself. My mom's vegetarian bologna tastes like nothing you've ever put in your mouth. Let's just say it's round, ground, pinkish leaves of grass. Let's just say it's nonfood.

Ever since my mother took over Papa Pete's deli, she has been experimenting like crazy with food. Unfortunately for me, my lunch is her laboratory. Vegetarian bologna is only one of her experiments. You haven't lived until you've tried her soy salami. Papa Pete says it's a crime what she does to salami.

By the way, Papa Pete is my grandpa. He's the best. Sometimes I get the feeling that he's the only person who understands me. He never ever thinks I'm stupid or lazy.

"Actually, bologna is a very interesting word," Robert said through a mouthful of macaroni and cheese.

Frankie and I looked at each other. You know how when you have a best friend, you and the other person often think the same thing at the same time? We were both thinking, Somebody get me out of this conversation!

"What's especially interesting is that bologna contains a silent *g*, just like the silent *k* in knock or knight," Robert went on.

Robert knows everything. That's why he skipped second grade. I think it's great to know a lot of things. I just don't think you have to say them all the time. Like Robert will name all the James Bond movies in order, including the year they came out, even when no one asks him. And don't even start him on world capitals. He'll tell you the capital of Indonesia right in the middle of a dodgeball game. The other day he just looked at me and said, "The human body has enough iron to make one nail." He said it like it was a totally normal thing to say!

"Robert," I said, "why don't you go sit with the third-graders."

"They're not interested in what I have to say," he said.

"We're not interested either," I said.

"Why not?" he answered. "Spelling is a very challenging subject."

"Challenging?" I said. "That's the understatement of the century. I can't spell to save my life. And it really bothers me, too."

"I can't imagine not being able to spell," Robert said. "Doesn't it make you feel stupid?"

"Robert, will you cut Zip a break?" said Frankie, giving him a noogie on the head. "Can't you see he's a troubled man?"

"What's wrong with you?" Robert asked.

"Ms. Adolf is making us write an entire five-paragraph essay," I answered. "Neatness counts. Punctuation counts. Everything counts. Do you realize how impossible that is?"

Just then, Ashley slid onto the bench next to

me and put her tray down. She had chosen both the mac and cheese and the tuna melt. Ashley likes variety—in everything. You should see her clothes. She covers them all with rhinestones—even her sneakers. She's got one pair with a family of dolphins swimming in the ocean, in blue and green rhinestones. She glues them all on herself.

"What's impossible?" asked Ashley.

"Spelling," I said.

"Spelling is hard," she agreed. "But this is impossible."

She picked up a cherry that was sitting on top of her fruit salad. She popped it into her mouth and ate it. Then her face got all twisted up and busy, like a chipmunk shelling an acorn. In no time, she stuck out her tongue and there was the cherry stem, tied in a perfect knot. Is Ashley Wong an amazing girl or what?

"Ashweena, that is so cool," said Frankie. Frankie has a nickname for everyone. He even calls my dad Mr. Z. No one else I know even *talks* to my father.

"Does nobody care about my problem?" I said. "Is anybody listening?"

My friends stopped eating and looked at me.

"How am I going to write five perfect paragraphs by next Monday when I can't get what I'm thinking about down on paper?" I said. "My handwriting looks like a chicken stepped in tar and ran across the page."

"If a chicken stepped in tar, it would get stuck and couldn't run anywhere," Robert pointed out.

"Shut up, Robert," we all said together.

"I put commas in the wrong places," I continued. "My capital letters look weird. My lowercase letters look even weirder. My spelling—well, we all know about my spelling."

"Take a breath, Zip," said Frankie. "We'll figure it out. Hey, make friends with the dictionary. Let your fingers do the walking, if you know what I'm talking about."

Frankie is really good at school. He thinks math is easy *and*, get this—he reads for fun. I wish I could do that. I wish it were easier for me to read a book.

"You sound just like my father," I said. "He's always telling me to look up words in the dictionary."

Suddenly, Frankie grabbed his chest and fell to the ground, flopping around like he was some kind of alien. He's cool enough to be able to do a thing like that in the lunchroom. Even Kate Sperling and Kim Paulson were laughing. Not at him, either, but with him.

"That hurts," he screamed. "Comparing me to Silent Stan, the crossword-puzzle man." (That's another one of Frankie's nicknames for my dad.) Frankie got up and sat back down at the table. "Someone, please. What's a four-letter word for a root vegetable?" he said, doing his perfect imitation of my father working a crossword puzzle.

We all cracked up. Milk came shooting out of Ashley's nose. It spewed all over her T-shirt, spraying the rhinestone self-portrait she had done. Drops of milk hung off of the purple stones she had used for the frames of her glasses.

"Does anyone have a napkin?" Ashley asked.

"Here, take mine," I told her. "My sandwich is never going to make it to my mouth anyway."

Frankie climbed back onto the bench.

"Do me a favor, Zip," he said. "Don't ever tell me that I sound like your father again."

"Then don't bring up the dictionary again," I said. "It's such a useless invention. At least for me."

"Don't tell that to Ms. Adolf," said Ashley. "She's in love with dictionaries."

"They don't make any sense," I said. "I can't spell words because I can't sound them out. So how am I going to find them in a dictionary if I can't spell them in the first place? Do you know my dictionary has one thousand two hundred and fifty-six pages? Words get lost in there."

"Zip, you're forgetting to . . ."

". . . breathe. I know, Frankie. I *am* breathing."

Frankie put his hand on my shoulder. "Look, it's just an essay, my man."

"Maybe for you," I said. "For me, it's torture."

Frankie reached into his lunch bag and pulled out a package of Ding Dongs. He took one for himself and gave one to me.

"Listen up, Zip," he said. "We're supposed to write about what we did on our summer vacation, right? So just write about what happened to you. You had an awesome summer vacation—going to Canada and to Niagara Falls and getting to steer the boat all by yourself when the captain fell overboard. Man, that's cool stuff."

Ashley nearly gagged on her second cherry stem.

"That's not what you told *me*," she said. "You told me your sister got seasick and barfed all over your plastic raincoat."

Okay, okay, so sometimes I tell stories. But they're not lies or anything. It's just that I think the world needs to be entertained. I happen to be good at it. Like Papa Pete says, "If you got it, flaunt it." Flaunt. There's another word I can't spell.

Suddenly, out of nowhere came a hand bigger than an average hand. Bigger than a tabletop. Then a head the size of Rhode Island appeared. Next came the smell of bad, bad breath—the kind that makes the gel in your hair lose its hold.

"That Ding Dong is mine," Nick McKelty said as he smashed what was once my chocolate cake into his oversized mouth. "I wuffofv deese."

Robert dove for cover under the table. Ashley shot milk again.

"Be my guest," I said. It was either that or have Nick the Tick pound my skull with his knuckles. Nick thinks that because he is the biggest guy in the fourth grade, everybody's lunch is his personal meal. We are his menu and he just takes whatever he wants.

Nick was looking for his second course. My instincts told me he was headed for Ashley's tuna melt.

"Nick!" I said, yelling to catch his attention. "You don't want to eat that."

"Like you're going to stop me," he said, flashing me his stupid grin. The Ding Dong chocolate was wedged in the gap between his teeth so it looked like he had three front teeth.

"Did you hear about the tuna they just caught off Cape Cod that ate a license plate from a car from Ohio?" I said to him, thinking fast. "There was so much metal ground up inside him that by the time he got to the store he didn't need a can."

I pointed to Ashley's sandwich. "That's him in there."

You could almost hear the small wheels grinding inside his huge blond head.

"I didn't want that pathetic sandwich anyway," he said. "I've got to save my appetite for the Knicks' game tonight. My dad's got tickets right next to the players' bench."

Nick's father owns the bowling alley in our neighborhood, McKelty's Roll 'N Bowl. Maybe that's why Nick the Tick thinks he has the right to act like a big shot all the time. All he does is brag, and none of it is ever true.

Okay, like I said before, I tell stories sometimes too. But let's get one thing straight: My stories are for pure entertainment purposes. Nick's stories are to make him seem cool. Which he's not, I might add. Like he says his father has the best seats for every sporting event in the United States of America. The truth is, mostly they watch the games on the TV at the bowling alley. That's what we call The McKelty Factor. Truth times a hundred.

In any case, Nick walked away.

Ashley smiled at me. "Thanks, Hank," she said.

I felt proud. I had saved her lunch.

"You are amazing, Zip, " Frankie said. "You have so much trouble with so many things, but never with your mouth. It's a brilliant mouth."

I thought about that. If my brilliant mouth worked on Nick McKelty, why couldn't it work on Ms. Adolf?

I took out a piece of paper and a pencil. I had a plan.

CHAPTER 4

BEFORE LUNCH ENDED, I decided to find Ms. Adolf and have a little chat. She was sitting at her desk, finishing her lunch. Two big napkins covered most of her. Just her shoes were showing. They were gray. She was eating a banana that was so brown you couldn't even tell it had ever been yellow.

"May I talk with you for a minute, Ms. Adolf?" I asked from the doorway.

She waved me inside.

"I've been thinking a lot about my essay," I began.

"I'm glad to hear that, Henry," she said.

"What I've been thinking about, exactly, is that it would really benefit you if I don't write this essay."

"Is that so?" she said. She tossed the banana peel into the wastebasket.

"In fact, I've spent a good part of my lunch period writing a list of ten really excellent reasons why I shouldn't write this essay."

I pulled the piece of paper from my back pocket and flattened it out on her desk with the palm of my hand. There was a big, greasy smudge on it. And it really, really smelled like tuna fish. I have to admit it was pretty disgusting.

"Sorry," I said, trying to rub it off. "It was tuna-melt day. Just pretend it's a scratch-and-sniff."

I smiled. Ms. Adolf didn't.

That wasn't a good start, but I had to think positively. I stood very quietly while she read the list.

TEN REASONS WHY HANK ZIPZER SHOULD NOT WRITE A FIVE-PARAGRAPH ESSAY ON WHAT I DID THIS SUMMER

1. Every pen I own runs out of ink.
2. My thoughts are controlled by alien beings who make me write in a strange language.

3. We couldn't go anywhere over the summer because my dog had a nervous breakdown.
4. I'm highly allergic to lined paper.
5. When I write, my fingers stick together.
6. If I sit too long, my butt falls asleep and snores, which keeps my sister awake.
7. Every time I write an essay, my dog Cheerio eats it for breakfast before I can get to school. So why try?
8. My computer keyboard is missing eleven letters—v, c, t, s, m, and all the vowels including y and w.
9.
10.

The last two reasons were on the tip of my mind, but I just couldn't get them to the tip of my pencil.

Ms. Adolf put down the list and looked up at me. "This is very creative," she said.

Creative. Creative is good. My plan was working.

"I hope you'll use some of this creativity in your essay," she went on. "I look forward to hearing you read your written words on Monday morning."

Then she took my list, crumbled it up, and tossed it in the wastebasket. There was my creativity, I thought—stuck to the top of a brown banana peel.

CHAPTER 5

THREE, TWO, ONE. *Brrriinnngg*. The bell. After an endless afternoon of alphabetizing practice, the first day of fourth grade was finally over. Frankie and I looked at each other. We were free men.

Frankie, Ashley, and I ran downstairs and practically flew out the front door of the school building. Papa Pete was waiting outside to walk us home. Papa Pete is my mother's father. He also happens to be one of the greatest human beings on the face of the earth. He was helping Mr. Baker, the crossing guard, take the little kids across the street.

"There he is," said Frankie, waving to Papa Pete. "Get your cheeks ready."

When Papa Pete sees you, he gives you a big pinch and says, "I love this cheek and everything that's attached to it." I know this sounds

31

like it's annoying, but actually it makes you feel really good.

Papa Pete gave us each a pinch and a hug. "I hardly recognized you kids," he said. "You look so much older now that you're in the fourth grade."

We had hoped this was the year we'd be allowed to walk home from school by ourselves. After all, Frankie, Ashley, and I lived in the same apartment building, so we could all walk together. Safety in numbers, we all told our parents. But we were all turned down flat. New York City is not a place for kids to be wandering around alone, our parents said.

Okay, we could live with that, because having Papa Pete walk you home is actually pretty fun. He walks ten feet behind us to make it *look* like we're walking alone. Papa Pete is so big that there was no way we could lose him in a crowd, even if we tried. It's not that he's tall, he's just large the way a grizzly bear is large. My Grandma Jennie used to call him her big, cuddly grizzly bear. Maybe that was because he also has a ton of curly black hair on his arms and a huge mustache he calls his handlebars. After he eats something messy, he'll always say, "Tell me, Hank. Do I have anything hanging off the old handlebars?" I always tell him if he does, because he doesn't want to be embarrassed.

We headed up Amsterdam Avenue. We walked a couple blocks and passed Harvey's, our favorite pizza shop. It's no wider than a hallway, but they have the greatest cherry cokes and pizza there. You can smell it blocks away.

"I say we stop in for a slice," Frankie said.

Papa Pete shook his head. "Hold on, partner. We got bigger bread to butter."

When Papa Pete says a thing like that, you don't argue. He's always got something great waiting for you.

We passed the man on the corner selling sunglasses. "Hey, gentlemen and lady," he said to us. "I got a special pair just for your face."

Ashley stopped to look at a pair of rhinestone-covered glasses, but Frankie and I pulled her away. You can't let Ashley get started on rhinestones or you'll be there all day. She's a complete rhinestone nut.

Messengers on bikes whizzed by us. Moms

coming back from the park pushed their babies in strollers. I love to see the babies' feet hanging out of the strollers. It always amazes me that inside their little bitty feet are big feet waiting to pop out and play baseball.

A couple blocks up, we passed my mom's deli, the one Papa Pete started. It's called The Crunchy Pickle. They serve sandwiches so high they have to be held together with a toothpick. I waved at Carlos, who works at the counter. I could see him shouting something, and even though I couldn't hear him, I knew he was saying, "Hey, Little Man."

"Hey, Big Man," I called back.

When we got to our apartment building, Frankie and Ashley started to go inside. Papa Pete steered them back onto the sidewalk.

"You haven't forgotten, have you? " he said. "We have some business to conduct. I was thinking maybe you could come to my office."

Papa Pete's "office" is McKelty's Roll 'N Bowl. It's his hangout, his home away from home. Everyone there knows him. He's the best senior bowler on the Upper West Side of Manhattan.

"I have to ask my parents," Ashley said.

"I took the liberty of phoning the good Doctors Wong," said Papa Pete, "and they said you don't have to be home until six." Although Ashley's parents are both doctors, Papa Pete is the only one I know who calls them "the good Doctors Wong." They don't seem to mind, though.

"I don't think my mom will let me go," Frankie said. "My dad teaches tonight and she likes me home."

Frankie's dad teaches African-American studies at Columbia University, which is thirty-eight blocks uptown. Once, his dad let me come to one of his lectures. He talked for almost two hours. I don't think I'll ever go to college if you have to sit still and listen to someone talk for two hours—and take notes at the same time.

"Fortunately for you, your mother was standing on her head when I called," Papa Pete said to Frankie, "so I spoke with your father. When I explained that we were discussing important business, he said okay."

That was all we needed to hear. We took off for McKelty's, which is only a couple blocks from our apartment building. It's located on the second floor above the ninety-nine-cent store, where I do most of my gift shopping. I bought my mom some earrings there for Mother's Day. She doesn't wear them much, though, because they hurt her lobes. Lots of people who shop at the ninety-nine-cent store don't even realize that there's a bowling alley upstairs. You can hardly see it from the street, but it's got fifteen lanes, video games, and a coffee shop, too.

When we got to McKelty's, the lanes were full of Papa Pete's friends. They were all wearing their different-colored team shirts. They waved to us as we took a seat in one of the red plastic booths in the coffee shop.

"Fern," Papa Pete called out. "Three root-beer floats for my grandkids here."

The fact that Frankie is African-American and Ashley's parents are from Taiwan doesn't stop Papa Pete from calling them his grandkids. That's another thing I love about him. And another is that he'll always buy you as many root-beer floats as you want without ever mentioning that they will ruin your appetite for dinner.

Fern, who has been working at McKelty's for like a hundred and fifty years, brought us our root-beer floats.

As we were slurping down the last of our ice cream, Papa Pete started talking. "Okay, let's get down to business," he said, wiping some whipped cream from his mustache. "I believe you've got a little something to show me."

I haven't mentioned this before, because sometimes I forget things, but Frankie is an outrageous magician. He doesn't just do the tricks you buy in the store, either. He makes up his own. Anybody can make a nickel disappear and then pull it out of your ear. But Frankie can make a *quarter* disappear and then have five nickels drop out of his nose. Now *that's* what I call *magic*.

Papa Pete was thinking about hiring him to be the entertainment at his Bowling League's Start of the Season Party. His team is called the Chopped Livers. Everything about Papa Pete has to do with the deli he used to own—like his two parakeets are named Lox and Bagels. I'm surprised he didn't name my mother Pickled Herring.

"Let's see what you can do," Papa Pete said to Frankie.

"You mean you're making the kid audition?" Fern said.

"Business is business," answered Papa Pete, winking at Ashley and pinching my cheek, all at the same time.

Frankie reached into his backpack, got out three red cups, and placed them in a row on the table.

"What you see before you are three ordinary red cups," he began. He took out two small and one medium royal blue sponge balls that he smushed together into the palm of his hand. He asked Ashley to blow on his closed hand three times, then opened his palm and the balls had transformed into one big blue sponge ball. He put that ball under the middle red cup. He moved all the cups around in a flurry, then put them in a stack.

"*Zengawii!*" chanted Frankie. It's a word he made up when he went to Zimbabwe with his parents a couple years ago. Frankie says it has magical powers.

He lifted the stack of cups high in the air.

There on the table were the two small and one medium sponge balls.

"You're hired," Papa Pete said as he applauded. "Do you want the job?"

"Could I have a word with my associates for a moment?" I asked Papa Pete. "In private."

I pulled Frankie and Ashley off to the side.

"I see a future here for us all," I said. "Frankie, you're the head magician, but you're going to need an assistant, which is me. And we'll need a business manager. That's you, Ashley. You'll make us millionaires."

"I want to be an assistant, too," Ashley said.

"Okay, " I said. "We'll switch off. But you still have to be the money person, because I'm dangerous with numbers." Last week, I went to buy a slice of pizza, and they were out of dollar bills, so the guy gave me change all in coins. I just had to trust that he gave me the right change, because there was no way I could add it all up in my head. I would have needed a pad of paper, a pencil, and my sister, Emily, who is like a human calculator, to figure it out.

"Okay," said Ashley. "Since I'm the business person, let me do the talking."

"Go for it, Ashweena," said Frankie, slapping her a high five.

We went back over to Papa Pete.

"In the last few minutes, we've formed a partnership," said Ashley. "We've considered your offer, and my partners and I believe that for seventy-five dollars, we can put on a magic show never to be forgotten."

"I believe," said Papa Pete, tugging on his mustache, "that for thirty dollars, you can put on a magic show that I'll like even better."

"Take it," I whispered in Ashley's ear. "It'll only go down from here."

"Deal," Ashley said. And she stuck out her hand.

Papa Pete shook it, and said, "And of course, for this kind of money, I'd hope to see a small live furry thing coming out of a top hat. I always enjoy that."

"No problem," Ashley said.

Frankie and I shot each other panicked looks. Why was she promising that? We didn't have a small live furry thing.

We grabbed Ashley by the arm and pulled her over to the video game room. I knew I had to get her away from Papa Pete before she agreed to make the Empire State Building disappear.

"What were you thinking?" I said to Ashley.

"I was thinking about a rabbit," she said. "It's always nice to pull a rabbit out of a hat."

"Earth to Ashley," said Frankie. "We don't have a rabbit."

"That's a good point," she said.

"Now what are we going to do?" I asked. "You promised Papa Pete we'd pull a live, furry thing out of a top hat! He's counting on it."

Ashley just smiled. "You'll think of something, Hank. You always do."

CHAPTER 6

ON THE WALK HOME, we couldn't stop coming up with names for our new magic business. When we left McKelty's, we thought The Magic Trio sounded really good. Smooth and simple. By the time we crossed the street, we had switched to something flashier, like The Three Magicteers. When we saw a neon sign in front of the all-night laundromat, we came up with Magic: Open All Night. By 83rd Street, Frankie was convinced we should be The Mystical Magical Dudes. By 82nd Street, Ashley was pushing for The Disappearing Act.

By the time we reached 78th street, we had decided. We were Magik 3. Frankie thought we definitely should spell Magic with a *k* because it looks cool. That was fine with me, since that's the way I thought it was spelled anyway.

It felt so great to have a name. And a plan.

We figured we'd start our career at McKelty's Roll 'N Bowl. Then we'd move on to kids' parties and get known all over the entire West Side. Next, we'd take our show downtown. And finally on to Madison Square Garden where there'd be thousands of fans, chanting our name: "Magik 3. Magik 3. Magik 3."

We decided to start rehearsals right away, so we scheduled a kickoff meeting right after dinner. I was so excited about Magik 3 that I couldn't wait to go upstairs and tell my parents about us. I buzzed our apartment number. My sister Emily answered the intercom.

"Who's there?" she asked.

"Open sesame," I said in my magician assistant's voice.

"Hank? Is that you? Why do you sound so weird?"

"The Mighty Zengawii requests that you let him in . . . in . . . in." I gave my voice this really cool echo. Frankie and Ashley cracked up.

"Mom," Emily yelled. "Hank's downstairs and he thinks he's being funny but he's not."

"Just buzz him in, honey," I heard my mom

say over the sound of the blender in the kitchen.

"I'm letting you in," Emily said. "But if it were up to me, I'd leave you standing down there until you act normal."

That's a strange thing to say coming from Emily, who's about as un-normal as a person can be.

Frankie, Ashley, and I got into the elevator and pressed our floors. I live on ten, which is the top floor. Frankie lives on six, and Ashley lives on four. As we rode up, I imagined the three of us dressed in black capes and top hats. We'd all have mustaches. Ashley would look so funny in a mustache. The elevator stopped at her floor. I pushed the door open and held it with my foot. We all put out hands out and placed them on top of one another's.

"Magik 3 rules," we chanted.

Ashley got out. Frankie and I headed for six.

"Watch this," said Frankie. He snapped his fingers and said, "Zengawii." The elevator stopped and the door opened on his floor.

I rode by myself up to ten. When I got out, I shoved my key into my apartment door lock and made my entrance into the apartment.

"Good evening, ladies and gentlemen of the Zipzer family," I said, with a sweep of my imaginary cape. "Welcome to the most astounding show you will ever behold, featuring the amazing talents of Magik 3! I am one of them."

I took a bow.

No one said a word.

My dog, Cheerio, ran up to me to say hello. At least someone in the family appreciated me. I took another bow. A really deep one. A really long one.

"I'm going to my room until dinner," Emily said. "This is too strange for me."

My father was sitting in his boxers at the dining room table, working a crossword puzzle. He was wearing a pair of glasses on the top of his head. He does that sometimes, even though I'm pretty sure he doesn't have eyes up there. He looked at me like I was a short stranger.

"You're late," he said.

"We were with Papa Pete at McKelty's."

"You should have called."

"But I was with Papa Pete. Not some stranger," I told him.

"You have to learn to be responsible,

Hank," he answered back.

Responsible? I'm a small-business owner. How much more responsible can you get? But I didn't tell my dad that.

"I'm sorry, Dad," I said. "I'll call next time."

My mother came in from the kitchen. I could tell she'd been cooking because her hair was pulled back with a headband. Her hair is blond and curly, and when she wears it loose, bits of food she's cooking sometimes land in it. She's had all kinds of things in her hair—flour, chunks of chocolate-chip cookie dough. Once, she even found a lima bean. The hairband is her new discovery, and it's been working really well for her.

Mom started to push my father's papers to the end of the dining room table. We eat at one end of the table, and his office is at the other. He does something with computers. I'm not sure what it is, but I know it's pretty boring.

"How was your first day, my big fourth-grader?" my mom asked, kissing me on the cheek. "Did you remember to bring home your assignment sheet?"

"That would be a first," said Emily the

Perfect. She came out of her bedroom carrying her iguana, Katherine, on her shoulder. Who names a lizard Katherine?

Some people say that Emily and I look alike. Even though she's fifteen months younger than me, we're almost the same size. We both have green eyes and dark hair that goes in a lot of different directions, like my Dad's. But as far as I'm concerned, that's where the similarity ends. For one thing, I don't polish each fingernail a different color like Emily does. And for another, I don't have to use Chap Stick all the time because I lick my lips too much. And most important, I don't walk around with an iguana on my shoulder.

My sister Emily calls herself a reptile person. I call her a *creepy* reptile person. I mean, you're trying to enjoy your dinner and all of a sudden, her iguana snaps its long tongue out and snatches a carrot off your plate. How can a guy digest? And my parents don't say anything. Not a word!

My mom went back to the kitchen and brought out some soup for dinner. It was barley mushroom. I could tell it was Papa Pete's recipe because it smelled great. She dished everyone up a big bowl, took off her headband and apron, and sat down at the table.

"Who wants to share their day?" Mom asked. She says this every night at dinner. The great thing is that she really wants to hear all about your day.

I let Emily start.

"Who do you think got appointed eraser monitor?" she said. "Me. And our teacher, Miss Springflower, said I have the neatest penmanship she's ever seen. And she was really impressed with my summer reading list. She said she's never met a not-even third-grader who could read a three hundred twenty nine-page book. I think I'm her favorite, and it's only the first day."

The only thought that came to my mind was, Could you barf?

The iguana's elastic tongue shot out for some soup. She missed, and her tongue made the soup splash high out of the bowl, hitting my father smack in the eye.

"Emily, take that thing and put it back in your room," he said.

Finally, he was reacting in a normal way.

"This so-called thing is an iguana whose natural habitat is the Galapagos," Emily said.

"So, can we FedEx it back home?" I asked.

My father chuckled.

"Stanley," said Mom. "Katherine is a member of this family, too."

"And what am I?" said my dad. "A lowly fly on the wall?"

I love it when adults say things like that—things that sort of make sense but don't really.

"Let's not spoil a nice dinner," said my mom. She turned her attention to me. I was crumbling a cracker into my soup. I like to float the pieces, watch them get soggy, and eat them just before they sink.

"Hank," said my mom. "It's your turn. Let's hear about your day."

"My teacher, Ms. Adolf, is so strict," I began. "We have to write a *huge* essay about what we did on our summer vacation. Five paragraphs."

No sooner were the words out of my mouth than I knew I had made a big mistake. My father wanted to know when it was due. My

49

mother wanted to know when I was planning to start. Knowing me, they both suggested I begin tonight.

"I want to start on it, because you know how much I believe in getting an early start on things," I said with my fingers crossed. "But tonight I have a very important meeting at the clubhouse at seven."

"Honey, you know how long it takes you to do your homework," said my mother.

"This is the first assignment of the year," added my father. "You have to make a good impression on your teacher."

"But my business partners are counting on me," I pleaded.

"What business partners?" my father asked, getting irritated.

"Now, Henry," my mother said.

Uh-oh. The H-word. Whenever she calls me Henry, I know it's all over.

"We talked about starting this school year off on the right foot. I know you want to do that, don't you?"

"But I have six whole days to write it," I said. "That's less than a paragraph a day.

And this meeting could change my entire life. And yours."

"That's enough," my father said. "Right after dessert, you're going to march into your room, sit down at your desk, and start writing. I want one paragraph completed tonight."

Just then, Katherine flipped out her disgusting tongue and snapped up the last piece of cracker that I'd been saving.

This night was going nowhere fast.

CHAPTER 7

I LOVE MY ROOM and I hate my room.

My bunk bed can be turned into a fort. All I have to do is tuck the blankets under the top mattress and let them hang down to the floor. I sleep on the bottom bunk and my desk is directly across from the window. Everything is where I want it to be. My clock radio is by my bed. My CD player is portable, so it can move to where I need it. Inside my closet I have a secret panel where my old cigar box holds the most important items on Earth. There's a dollar bill that Mom gave me for helping to clean up our dog's poop, a red star that my first-grade teacher gave me for telling the best story, my very first Hot Wheels car—a silver Ferrari F-50 convertible that I named Shiny, a bunch of baseball cards that will be very valuable some-day, and . . . that's pretty much it.

Those are the things I love about my room. What I hate about my room is that's where homework calls to me day and night like a monster. "Finish me. Finish me. Pick up your pencil."

I sat down at my desk and took out a piece of lined paper. Let's not forget that I'm allergic to lined paper. But I was determined to concentrate and get some of my essay done.

Cheerio ran into my room. He started to spin around in a circle. Now let me ask you this: How can a guy concentrate when his dog spends most of his waking hours chasing his tail? Cheerio, who is a very long dachshund, has been trying to catch his tail since he was a puppy. That's how he got his name. He's beigeish-brownish. So is a Cheerio. He looks like a circle. So does a Cheerio. Sometimes he spills his milk on himself, and then he looks like a bowl of Cheerios.

Watching Cheerio spin is like watching clothes twirling around in the dryer. It's boring, and you try to look away. But somehow you're just sucked in.

I was finally able to unhook my eyes from

Cheerio and look at my desk. The lined paper stared up at me. My pencil was sharpened and ready. So why couldn't I just pick it up and write . . . something . . . anything? The piece of paper seemed like it was spinning around the desktop . . . like my dog. I pushed my hand straight out to stop it. My thoughts were spinning. *Niagara Falls . . .* I wrote that down. At last, something was coming. *My family is in raincoats and boots and rain hats.* We had to rent them. I wrote that down, too.

All of a sudden, I looked down and saw that my desk drawer was open a crack. My hand just shot down and pulled it open even further. Boy, was it a mess! How did that happen? I felt this powerful need to straighten up everything in my drawer.

My broken watch collection was all over the place. My special marbles had rolled all the way to the back. I took some Scotch tape and taped the marbles down. I was on fire! Then I noticed that the ballpoint pens had somehow gotten into the pencil part of the divider. I couldn't have that.

"Henry Zipzer, are you writing your essay?" my mother called from outside my door.

I slammed the drawer shut and picked up my pencil.

"You bet, Mom."

I looked down at the paper. I squinted my eyes and saw a sentence and a half—that's all I had written. I looked at my clock radio. We had a seven o'clock meeting in our clubhouse down in the basement. How was I going to make it? I'd never get out of my room. I hated my room. I hated my assignment. I hated my brain. Why couldn't I think or write or spell or add or divide? Forget about multiplying.

It's not like I don't try. I do. I go over and over and over my times tables and my vocabulary lists. My sister tests me, and I know everything. But then comes the test, and I can't remember them. It's like my mind is a chalkboard and the words just slide off it in the time it takes to walk from my apartment building to school, which is a block and a half away. It makes me so mad that sometimes I hit my head with my fist, hoping I'll start everything working again.

The piece of paper was still there in front of me. Still pretty much empty. I picked up my pencil and reread my sentence and a half. Great. I spelled Niagara wrong. Erasing was a trick. My eraser ripped the paper to shreds. As I moved it over the sheet of notebook paper, a hole started to appear. Small at first, and then it grew. It finally got so big, I could see the desktop through it.

I wadded up the sheet of paper and tossed it. It hit the rim of my wastepaper basket. Mom and Dad gave it to me for my birthday last year, and they put family pictures all around the outside under plastic.

Start again, Hank, I told myself. Think. *Niagara Falls . . . or Does It?* by Hank Zipzer.

I wondered if the title could be considered a paragraph?

Probably not.

CHAPTER 8

"MAN, ARE YOU LATE!" Frankie said, a little bit angry. "It's seven-thirty."

"We thought you weren't coming," Ashley piped in.

"Hey, I didn't think I was coming," I snapped back. "Parent problems."

"I happen to know that your mom isn't even home," said Frankie. "I know that because she's upside-down in my living room."

"My dad went to yoga class tonight too," said Ashley. "He said he needed to de-stress. I'd be stressed too if I had to look at pictures of people's disgusting insides all day."

"We gotta get my dad to go to yoga," I said. "He could definitely use some de-stressing. He wouldn't even let me come here tonight until I wrote a paragraph of my essay."

"Did you get one?" asked Ashley.

"Yeah, I wrote a paragraph."

"Great," said Ashley, throwing an arm around me.

"Then I erased it."

"Not so great." Ashley looked worried.

"I assume you didn't mention the erasing part to Silent Stan," said Frankie.

"He didn't ask, and I didn't tell."

I don't lie to my parents, but I have to confess, there are times when I don't spill everything. I think you know what I mean.

I fell backward into one of the sofas that lined the wall of our clubhouse. Cheerio, who had come with me, started to sniff the place out. He always sniffs around like he's going to find something new. He never does, but as long as he doesn't lift his leg, I figure he can do whatever he wants.

Our clubhouse is in the basement of our apartment building. When you get off the elevator, you start smelling soap suds because the laundry room is to the right. But if you turn to the left, there are three rooms with padlocks on them filled with stuff everyone who lives in the building doesn't want. Old chairs and sofas and bird cages, suitcases of every size, boxes of books and food magazines. A lot of parent kind of stuff.

One of the rooms doesn't have a lock so we use it for our hideout. It's a perfect meeting spot. Well, almost perfect. It would be totally perfect if Robert didn't know about it.

Ashley and Frankie had already made a list of the tricks Frankie was going to do for Papa Pete's show. It said:

1. Take nickels from nose
2. Transform one scarf into many scarves
3. Make thumb disappear
4. Pull live furry thing from hat

"Numbers one through three are no-brainers," Frankie said, "but number four isn't going to happen. We'd better face it now."

"But I promised Papa Pete," said Ashley. "I shook on it."

"Fine," said Frankie. "Then you've got to find me something live and furry."

"How about Robert?" I suggested.

"No," said Frankie. "His mother would

freak out if we try to stuff him in a hat."

Cheerio got tired of sniffing and started to chase his tail.

"Cheerio's at it again," Ashley said. "Doesn't he ever get dizzy?"

I looked at Cheerio twirling around like a top. A flash of inspiration hit me. Cheerio! He was small. He was furry. He was alive.

"Members of Magik 3," I said as I sprang off the sofa. "I have the answer. We're pulling Cheerio out of that hat."

When he heard his name, Cheerio stopped spinning for a minute and looked me right in the eye. Then he started spinning again.

Frankie put his hand to his forehead, like he had a bad headache. "He does that inside a hat and I'm telling you right now, he'll burn a hole in the fabric."

"Cheerio can be calm," I said. "He'll cooperate."

"Right, and my name is Bernice," said Frankie. "By the way, here's another question, guys. What top hat have you ever seen that this dog would fit in?"

"He's our best choice, Frankie. He's also our

only choice," Ashley said. "So we'll just have to figure out a way." She pushed her glasses up on her nose, and folded her arms in a way that meant business. Ashley can be tough when she wants to be.

"I think we can build a hat big enough to hold Cheerio," I suggested. "There's stuff all over here that we could use."

"Yeah, like what?" Frankie asked.

I looked around. On the shelf above the door, I saw a big, round hatbox kind of thing. We pulled it down, took off the top, and put Cheerio inside. He fit perfectly.

"Great, we'll use this," I said. "We'll cover it in black felt."

"Like we happen to have a big pile of felt lying around," Frankie said.

"I know where they sell felt." I had just seen some the week before in the ninety-nine-cent store. It was in the school supplies section.

"It's still not going to look like a hat," said Frankie.

"Then we'll get some cardboard and make a brim," I answered.

"That sounds hard," said Ashley. "How will

we get the brim to stick on?"

"Trust me," I said. "I'm a genius with super glue."

"Okay, genius," said Frankie. "Tell me how we're going to keep your nutcase dog inside the hat until it's time to pull him out?"

"I'll build a pocket inside and put some biscuits there, to keep Cheerio calm." By now, Frankie and Ashley were pretty impressed with my ideas. I have to admit, I was too.

"We can even put the whole hat on wheels," I said. I don't know where that idea came from. It just popped into my mind. One second there was nothing in my head, and the next second there was a hat on wheels. It was amazing.

"Hank, you are covered in creativity," Ashley said.

"You're the second person today who's used that word," I said to her. "Ms. Adolf told me she was looking forward to seeing me use my creativity in my essay."

Then it struck me. Creativity. It was the answer to all my problems. Creativity solved our hat problem. And creativity was going to get me through Ms. Adolf's essay. And not just get me through, either. My creativity was going to get me the best grade of my life.

Let everyone else write their stupid five paragraphs. Not me. Right then and there, I decided I was going to *build* my essay. I'd *bring* Niagara Falls into the classroom, water and all.

I could see it in my mind, just like I saw the big hat for Cheerio. I'd build a living model of Niagara Falls, with the cliffs and waterfalls and even a boat. Everyone would know firsthand what I did on my summer vacation. Principal Love would hear about how great it was and come to our classroom just to see it. He'd call my dad and say what a great job I had done.

Papa Pete always says, "There are many roads to Rome." I used to think he was talking about the traffic in Italy. But now it made sense to me. What he meant was, if you can't get there one way, take another way. Like if you can't pull a rabbit out of a hat, pull a dachsund out. And if you can't write about Niagara Falls, build it.

My brain was on fire, and it felt good.

CHAPTER 9

Do you know what lucky is? Lucky is having friends who understand that building a magic hat can wait when Niagara Falls needs to be built right away. Lucky is having friends who don't make you feel stupid even though that's how you think of yourself. Friends who don't make fun of you because some things—well, a lot of things—are hard.

I am so lucky.

As soon as I told Frankie and Ashley my idea about building Niagara Falls instead of writing the essay, they both volunteered to help.

"This is a big project," I said.

"We better make a list of supplies we'll need," Ashley suggested. "Frankie, you get a pencil and write the list."

"No way," said Frankie. "I'm not a secretary. I'm a builder. A hammer-and-nails kind of guy."

"When was the last time you built anything?" Ashley asked him.

"Kindergarten," said Frankie. "Remember that awesome gingerbread house I made out of milk cartons and graham crackers?"

"I remember that it collapsed and then you ate it," I said.

"Okay, you win. Hand me the pencil," Frankie said.

"The first thing we're going to need is water," I said. "Lots and lots of water."

"Newspaper and flour to build the cliffs," added Ashley.

"Twigs to make trees out of," I said.

"And rhinestones for the stars in the sky," said Ashley.

Frankie stopped writing.

"This isn't a T-shirt, Ashweena. Keep in mind, we are building one of the natural wonders of the world. Rhinestones have no place here."

"Then how about rocks for the cliffs," suggested Ashley.

"Rocks are good," said Frankie. He added rocks to the list.

"Let's put a boat at the bottom of the falls," I said. "I must have a toy boat somewhere. And maybe I can get a spare pump from one of Emily's old fish tanks."

"What do you need a pump for?" asked Frankie.

"Something's got to push the water over the falls," I said.

"We better have a pan to collect the water," said Ashley. "A big pan."

I asked everyone to gather as much stuff as they could and meet the next night to begin building. We were all pretty excited—until we turned to leave, that is. Then we saw the worst thing you could possibly find in the doorway. Robert.

"Hi guys," he said with a grin. "Good news. My mom says I can join the meeting."

I've got to remember to tell his mother he's not invited.

"What are you guys doing?" he asked.

"Fourth-grade stuff," answered Frankie. "You wouldn't understand."

"Try me."

"We're building Niagara Falls," I said.

"More than six hundred thousand gallons of water flow over Niagara Falls every second," Robert said.

"How do you know that?" Ashley asked.

"Actually, it's all up here," Robert said, pointing to his head.

"Clear your throat, Robert," said Frankie.

A lot of times, Robert gets this really annoying bubble in his throat when he talks, like he's got a little ball of slobber down there. He'll just go right on talking if you don't tell him to clear that thing out.

"I bet you won't be able to create the mist," Robert went on. "Did you know that Niagara Falls produces enough mist to fill half the Grand Canyon every twenty minutes?"

Ashley thought for a minute. "As much as I hate to admit it, the mist does sound important," she whispered to me.

This gave Robert all the encouragement he needed. "My mom has a fan she puts in the window on really hot days. We could use it to blow the water around to look like mist. I think she'd let us borrow it."

Oh great. Now it was *us*.

The next morning, I waited until Emily was in the shower and went into her room. In her closet, I found an old pump left over from when she had her Japanese fighting fish. I put the pump in a paper bag, along with a LEGO boat from my toy chest. Then I went into the kitchen to find a pan. As I was clanking around in the closet, my mom came in.

"Hi honey. What are you looking for?"

"That big pan you cook turkey in on Thanksgiving."

"Oh, I loaned it to Mrs. Fink. She was making a turkey for her son-in-law's birthday. Come to think of it, she never returned it."

"If it's okay with you, I'm going to get it back from her," I said. "I need it for a school project."

"Be sure to ask her how the turkey turned out," my mom said, as she put water on for tea. "I suggested she stuff it with wheatgrass and bean sprouts. I'm sure it was delicious."

I went next door to Apartment 10B and knocked on the door. Mrs. Fink answered. She isn't a small woman, and in her pink bathrobe, she looked like one of those giant pink elephants in the cartoons.

"Hankie!" she said. "Come in for a doughnut. I'll put my teeth in."

"That's okay, Mrs. Fink," I said. "I have to get to school. I was just wondering if I could get our turkey pan back."

"Of course, darling," she said. She went to the kitchen and came back with the pan. As she handed it to me, Mrs. Fink smiled and I thought I saw her gums. I took the pan and ran, without asking about the turkey.

After school, I took all my stuff to our clubhouse. Frankie brought a big stack of newspapers. Ashley had a box of rocks and pebbles she had collected at Riverside Park. Even good old Robert showed up with a fan.

There's a sink in the broom closet down the hall, and I filled the turkey pan halfway with water. We let Robert do most of the newspaper shredding. Ashley and I soaked the paper and mixed it with flour to make papier-mâché. As we built the cliffs, Ashley reminded me that we had to make a hole for the hose that was going to bring the water to the top of the falls.

The next day, we made another batch of papier-mâché and added it to the cliffs. A couple times, the cliffs got so high that the papier-mâché slid down to the bottom. I had to prop it up while Ashley held her hair dryer up to it. Even then, it took two whole days and nights for the cliffs to dry.

Finally, the cliffs were ready for us to decorate. We put rocks and pebbles around to make them look real. Frankie had snipped some branches off the ficus tree in his living room when his mother wasn't looking. We stuck those along the top of the cliffs to look like trees.

On Saturday night, I decided it was time to add the water part. I had been collecting cardboard tubes from our apartment. Three came from rolls of paper towels and a couple others were from bathroom tissue. I love saying "bathroom tissue." It rolls off your tongue. Not like "toilet paper," which sounds too much like what it actually is.

If I do say so myself, I had come up with a great plan to get the water to the falls. I was going to connect the tubes with waterproof tape. Then I'd wrap the outside of this cardboard snake with Saran wrap. We'd hook one end up to the hole we'd made in the cliffs, and the other end up to the faucet in the cleanup sink in our classroom. Connect the pump, turn on the water, and presto, Niagara Falls.

"What are you doing?" asked Frankie, when he saw me wrapping the tubes in Saran wrap.

I told him my brilliant plan.

"I don't know, Zip," he said, shaking his head. "Do you think that tube is going to be strong enough to hold water?

"Hey, if you can cover a bowl of watermelon with Saran wrap and turn it upside down, then this will hold too," I assured him. "I tell you water is going to sail through this baby."

On Sunday night, we had one final meeting to finish the project. I glued more trees onto the cliffs and put little LEGO people into the boat. Ashley and I carefully attached the hose. We painted the cliffs brown—or, as Robert pointed out, burnt sienna. He's a real pain about vocabulary, that guy, but I have to admit, he was very helpful.

When Niagara Falls was finished, we all stood back to admire it.

"Don't move," Frankie said. "I'll be right back."

He disappeared. Two minutes later, he was back, panting. He had run up six flights of stairs to his apartment. When he's on a mission, Frankie never waits for the elevator. He reached into his pocket and pulled out a gleaming baby blue stone that I recognized right away. It was his best piece of turquoise from his private rock and mineral collection. Frankie put a spot of glue on it and placed the turquoise on top of the cliff.

"It's got good karma," he said.

He gave me his classic Big Dimple smile, then put out his hand. We did our secret handshake.

"You're going to knock 'em dead, Zip."

Didn't I tell you I was lucky?

CHAPTER 10

THAT NIGHT, it was hard to sleep because I was so excited. I couldn't wait until morning when I'd take Niagara Falls to school and show everyone my living essay.

I heard the door creak open. My mom stuck her head in.

"All set for school tomorrow?" she asked.

"Yup."

"Are you sure you're finished with your essay?" she whispered.

"It couldn't be any more complete, Mom."

"Do you need me to proofread it?"

"I'm telling you, Mom, it's perfect."

"I love you," she said.

"Me too," I said.

And she closed the door.

I stared up at the ceiling. All I could think about were the incredible things that were going to happen to me after I showed Niagara Falls. I made a list in my head.

TEN INCREDIBLE THINGS THAT WILL HAPPEN AFTER EVERYONE SEES MY NIAGARA FALLS PROJECT

BY HANK ZIPZER

1. I won't get just an *A* on it, I'll get the highest *A* they've ever given in America.
2. Ms. Adolf will finally smile. (I wonder if her face will crack.)
3. They'll call an assembly for everyone in the school to see my project. Newspaper reporters will come. Television stations will bring their cameras.
4. I'll interview Frankie and Ashley on television. Maybe even Robert. Hmmm . . . no, not Robert.
5. The mayor of Niagara Falls will come to shake my hand.
6. Principal Love will declare a school holiday in my honor.
7. I'll be called to the White House to show my project to the president.

8. The president will be so impressed, he'll pass a law that kids in the fourth grade no longer have to write essays.

9. Every fourth-grade student in the country will break their number-two pencils in half.

10. Just before they do, they will all write me letters to say thank you. I'll have to get a secretary just to answer my fan mail.

11. I will never have to clear the table again. Emily, on the other hand, will have to do it until she's fifty-six.

I fell asleep with a smile on my face.

CHAPTER 11

OKAY, ABOUT THE LIST in the last chapter. You're right. There are eleven things on it and I said there were only going to be ten. Well, you shouldn't be surprised. It's me, Hank Zipzer. I'm lucky that all my fingers and toes are attached. Otherwise, I'd lose count.

CHAPTER 12

WHEN MY ALARM CLOCK rang the next morning, I didn't hear the buzzer. All I heard was, "Monday morning, Monday morning, Monday morning." It was going to be tricky getting Niagara Falls to school, so we had to leave extra early. Ashley said her mom had to be at the hospital anyway, so she didn't mind walking us to school.

We met in the basement. Frankie and I each picked up one end of the pan. Since it was my project, I volunteered to be the one who walked backward. Ashley took the water pump, the Saran-wrapped hose, and a paper bag with my costume in it. (I haven't mentioned the costume before, because I threw it in at the last minute. I thought it would add what Papa Pete calls "pizazz.")

When we got outside our building, Ashley cleared the people out of the way and kept watch for big cracks in the sidewalk so I wouldn't trip. First we passed by Mr. Kim's market. He was putting out buckets of fresh flowers for the day. When he saw Niagara Falls, he took a flower from one of the buckets and put it on the top of the cliffs.

"Flowers grow on mountain top," he said.

"Thanks, Mr. Kim," I said.

We reached the corner and waited for the light to change. When it was green, we crossed Amsterdam Avenue. A couple cab drivers blew their horns as we walked by, probably because they were so amazed to see Niagara Falls passing by right in front of them. I felt good because a lot of them had probably never been to Niagara Falls, and at least now they were getting a chance to see it.

"Please! Hold your honks!" I shouted, as I took a half bow. "And thank you, one and all."

Frankie started to laugh, and then I did too. Ashley knew we were heading into one of our marathon laughing fits. When we were little, she watched us get plenty of time-outs in school because of our uncontrollable laughter.

"Stop it, boys!" she said. "Concentrate. You don't want to drop it now."

"Children, don't dawdle in the intersection," Ashley's mom said. She had a good point. You can't fool around in a New York intersection. When the light changes, the cars go. If you're in the way, it's your problem.

Dr. Wong is very nice but very quiet. Ashley says she doesn't talk much because most of the people she is around all day are asleep. She's a surgeon.

We made it to the school crosswalk without falling, tripping, or dropping the project. We only had a few more steps to go, but they were tricky ones. There are a couple big potholes in front of our school. They're always fixing them, but then other ones pop up. I heard once that potholes happened in the winter when there is ice and snow. Or maybe it's the traffic. No, I think it's the weather. When Emily was in kindergarten, I told her they were dragon foot-prints. Of course, it didn't scare her because, as we all know, she likes reptiles.

Our school is three stories high. On the

street side of the building, the bricks are covered with a big mural painted by some local New York artists. It shows a lot of happy kids with books open, sitting and reading happily under a rainbow. They sure didn't use me as a model.

When the traffic was clear, Mr. Baker, the crossing guard, took us across the street.

"That's a mighty fine looking mountain you got there," he said to us.

"It's Niagara Falls, sir," I said.

"Well it's a mighty fine looking Niagara Falls."

That made me feel good. Even though Mr. Baker says nice things to all the kids, I like to think he really did like our project.

Finally, we reached the main door of PS 87. There were kids swarming all around the school, and we had to be careful not to get crunched. We were attracting a lot of attention.

"Keep your distance," I said to a bunch of first-graders who were hovering around us. "Important fourth-grade business coming through."

Ashley held the door open for us and we

backed into the hall. We started the long climb to the second floor and our classroom. As luck would have it, the first person we saw when we got to the top was Nick McKelty.

"What is *that* supposed to be?" he asked in his usual creepoid manner.

I wasn't going to let this guy get to me.

"You just might be the only person in New York not to get it," I said. "We totally stopped traffic on Amsterdam Avenue. The taxis honked like we were a float in the Thanksgiving Day parade."

"Oh yeah?" McKelty said. "I was asked to ride on a float this year."

"Right, and my name is Bernice," Frankie said.

"In fact," McKelty went on, "they wanted me to be Santa Claus in the parade, but I said, 'Sorry, I'm already booked. Maybe next year.'"

"Breathe," Frankie said to himself. Then he turned to McKelty. "That's good," Frankie said, "because your face would've scared all those little kids. It's such a drag seeing kids cry at a parade."

"Oh yeah?" McKelty answered.

"What a comeback," said Ashley. "You're quick, McKelty."

From around the corner, we heard the squeak, squeak, squeak of rubber on linoleum. That could only be Principal Love. He always wears these black rubber-soled shoes that close with two Velcro straps. I guess he never learned to tie his laces.

"What have we here?" he boomed in his tall-man-bushy-hair voice.

We put Niagara Falls down on the floor.

"My summer vacation," I answered.

Nick stepped right in front of me.

"Our assignment is to do a five-paragraph essay on what we did this summer," said Nick. He gave Principal Love a smile that any sane person would describe as very, very icky. "*My* adventure was so exciting that *my* essay turned out to be *eight* paragraphs. And that's cutting it down from ten."

"Mr. McKelty, you've got a future." Principal Love grinned. Then he turned to me. "And as for you, Mr. Zipzer, don't be late for class."

He squeaked off down the hall. McKelty ran

after him, continuing to blab in his ear—probably telling him how much he happens to love Velcro straps on shoes.

"Don't be late," I muttered under my breath. "Where does he think I'm going? To the cafeteria for a big breakfast?"

"Forget him," said Ashley. "You've got to keep your mind on what you're doing here."

I could still see McKelty walking down the hallway, talking to Principal Love like he was his best friend. Then I saw something truly disgusting.

"I don't believe it," I said. "McKelty's putting his arm around him!"

The McKelty Factor strikes again.

The bell rang and Nick came lumbering down the hallway toward us. Just before he turned into the classroom, he stopped and looked at me.

"I have a wonderful surprise in store for you, Zippity Zipzer," he said.

He gave me an annoying flick under the chin, and slithered into class like the slimy snake he is.

CHAPTER 13

MS. ADOLF WAS on the prowl. She was hungry for paper.

"Please take your essays out, class," she said. "I hope you remembered to staple them in the upper-left-hand corner."

She walked up and down the aisles, clutching her roll book close to her chest. When she stopped at my desk, I could feel her hot breath on my head.

"Your desk appears to be empty, Mr. Zipzer," she said.

My heart was pounding. This was the moment.

"I thought we agreed you were to read your composition first," she snapped.

"And I am completely, totally prepared, Ms. Adolf," I said.

I looked at Frankie. I gave him a nod. He

gave Ashley a nod. The three of us stood and went to our planned positions.

Ashley took the Saran-wrapped tube and attached it with tape to the faucet at the cleanup sink. Frankie and I disappeared into the hall.

"Excuse me!" Ms. Adolf shouted. I think she was starting to get angry.

I stuck my head back into the classroom and said, "Get ready for creativity like you've never seen before."

Out in the hall, we got my costume out of the paper bag. Frankie held the yellow raincoat for me to slip into, and I pulled on the boots and the fisherman's hat. Then we picked up the project and walked it into the classroom, where we placed it on the sink counter.

"Exactly what do you think you're doing?" Ms. Adolf demanded to know.

"What you're about to see, Ms. Adolf, is what I did on my summer vacation. My living essay."

The kids moved closer so they could see. Ryan Shimozato even stood up on his chair. Katie Sperling and Kim Paulson were whispering to each other and giggling. I noticed that

Nick McKelty kept looking at the door to the classroom, like he was expecting someone.

Before Ms. Adolf could object again, I began.

"Niagara Falls was formed twelve thousand years ago, but when I visited this summer, it didn't look a day over eleven thousand. It did, however, look wet—really wet."

That was Ashley's cue. She turned on the faucet at the sink. With a quick twist of the nozzle, the water started to run through our hose and into the hole at the top of the papier-mâché cliff. I was so excited I couldn't continue. The falls were actually doing what they were supposed to do . . . falling! The water hitting the bottom of the turkey pan sounded like rain.

Ashley turned on the fish tank pump and it started to bubble, moving the water from the bottom of the turkey pan back up to the top of the falls. The boat at the bottom of the pan rose in the water. It was floating! Everything was working!

"Seven hundred and fifty thousand gallons of water flow over these falls every second," I said. Old Robert had finally come in handy.

"Do you see that boat?" I asked, pointing to the LEGO people in it. "Picture my mother, my father, my sister, and me—dressed as I am now, covered with mist."

At that moment, Frankie turned on the fan, and a little of the water started to blow toward my raincoat. The kids gasped.

"Awesome," said Ryan Shimozato.

"Truly awesome," said Justin, Ricky, and Gerald. They're Ryan's crew, and they like whatever he likes.

"Half the falls are in Canada, and the other half are in the United States, making Niagara Falls a link between our two countries," I went on. I remembered the tour guide had said that while we were waiting in line to get on the boat. I was on a roll. There were so many facts I knew about Niagara Falls, I could've gone on until lunch or longer.

Out of the corner of my eye, I saw that Frankie was trying to get my attention. I glanced over at him. He whispered something, but I couldn't quite understand him. It sounded like "no peeking." I didn't know what he was talking about. I shrugged and went on.

"We left New York City on a muggy August morning," I said, pretending to be driving in a car. "My mother said it was so hot you could fry eggs on her knees."

The kids laughed. They were loving this. I really felt wonderful and successful. Maybe I'll be a stand-up comedian when I grow up, I thought. Take this show on the road. I looked at Frankie. He wasn't laughing. Why not?

Whatever he had been trying to say to me, he said again. "No peeking"? Was that it? I still couldn't understand him. He sure was flapping his arms around a lot.

Just then, the door swung open. In walked Leland Love. Wow, this was great. The principal *was* coming to see my project, just like I had hoped.

"Tourists from all over the world come to see Niagara Falls," I said. I was getting more and more confident by the minute. "A couple from Italy asked me to take their picture with the falls in the background," I added. I hadn't even planned to tell that part of the story. It just came out.

Suddenly, Frankie walked in front of me and

with an Italian accent said, "I thinka thesa falls are betta than SpaghettiOs."

The class howled.

"SpaghettiOs rule!" laughed Luke Whitman. "SpaghettiOs forget-ios!" It doesn't take much for Luke to go out of control.

"What are you doing?" I whispered to Frankie. "You weren't supposed to talk."

"I've been trying to tell you," Frankie whispered. "We're leaking! Look!"

I looked over at the hose. Oh, no, this wasn't happening. The cardboard was soaking wet. The tube was turning to mush and the last piece of tape holding the hose to the cliffs was coming loose. I yelled for Ashley to turn off the water. She ran to the sink, but she was so nervous, she turned the water on full force instead, which totally blew the hose off the project. Water sprayed everywhere, but mostly on Ms. Adolf. She opened her mouth to speak and got a mouthful of falls.

The hose started to spin around, and the kids all ran for cover, laughing and shouting. Ms. Adolf was so stunned, she just stood there. *Bam!* She got pelted again with a blast of water.

When she put her hands up to her face to block the water, her roll book fell to the floor. It landed in a puddle of water. She gasped and tried to reach for it, but Luke Whitman was running wild and stomped on it, pushing it completely under water.

Ms. Adolf stared at her roll book. The paper was absorbing water fast and turning into a soggy mess. She opened her mouth wide, like she was going to scream really loudly, but all that came out was a mouse-like "eeeeekkk."

Bam! The hose came around again and hit her with another shot of water. She was really wet now. It looked like she had just stepped out of the shower with her clothes on. The pile of gray hair that was always neatly pinned on top of her head fell down and looked like a horse's tail.

"The water!" Principal Love yelled. "Someone turn off the water!" The kids were all laughing pretty hard, so no one moved toward the sink. Principal Love bolted across the room. He had to push by Luke Whitman, who was leading a bunch of kids in a rain dance. There was so much water on the floor, the classroom looked like a pond. Pencils, crayons, Ms. Adolf's roll book, and even a tunafish sandwich in a Baggie floated by.

Principal Love sloshed over to the sink. As he reached the counter, he stepped on the Baggie. It exploded and the tuna sandwich squished out from under his shoe. It was a slippery mess. Principal Love went sliding on the sandwich like he was on water skis. The last thing I saw before he went swimming was his hand reaching for the counter with the turkey pan on it. As the pan tipped, the papier-mâché flew and the muddy, mushy Niagara Falls landed with a splat all over Mr. Love's face.

I didn't mean to laugh, but I couldn't stop. In fact, I was laughing so hard that I fell tush-first into the water. Then what do I see but Nick McKelty's hand reaching out to Mr. Love.

"Don't worry, sir," he said. "I'll save you."

Sometimes I think things happen the way they're supposed to, because Nick McKelty, suckup of the century, slipped too and went flying headfirst into the muck. When he came up for air, he looked like he had a papier-mâché chicken sitting on his head. He wiped off his face and leaned over to Principal Love.

"Didn't I tell you Zipzer was about to launch a disaster?" he said.

Oh, so *that's* why Principal Love came to class. McKelty, that rat, told him to come see me make a fool of myself. And stupid me thought it was because he heard I had a great project.

Principal Love didn't say a word. All he did was wag a finger at me. I knew what that meant.

"I'll see you in my office . . . now!"

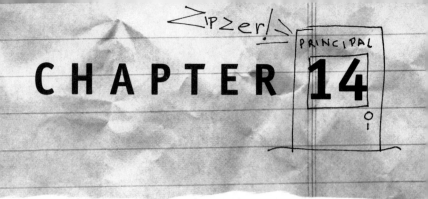

CHAPTER 14

THE HALLWAY IS a lonely place when you're sitting on the bench outside the principal's office. Kids you know walk by on the way to the bathroom or the water fountain, but no one says hello to you. No one even looks at you. It's like you're wearing a sign around your neck that says TROUBLE—KEEP AWAY.

I had been waiting in the hall for more than an hour. They were inside—the three of them, Principal Love and the Zipzers. That would be Stan and Randi. Also known as Mom and Dad.

It was hard to sit still. I got up and asked Mrs. Crock in the attendance office if I could have a pencil and paper, just to doodle or something.

"You're supposed to be using this time to think about what you've done," she said.

"I think better when I doodle," I told her.

"So do I," she said. She gave me a piece of paper and her pencil. That was nice of her.

When I went back into the hall, Principal Love was standing outside his office. He didn't speak—he just wagged his finger, inviting me in. It's the kind of invitation you don't say no to.

As I entered the office, I could tell my father was really angry. I knew that because his butt was hovering above the chair cushion, not quite touching it.

"Can I say something?" I said.

"Absolutely not," answered Principal Love. "I think your actions have spoken loudly enough."

I noticed that Principal Love's office smelled a little like tuna. It must be from his shoes, I thought. He had changed his shirt, but he still had a some papier-mâché stuck to his cheek. It was right above his Statue of Liberty mole. I couldn't help thinking that the Statue of Liberty finally had a torch.

"What you did today in class was completely irresponsible," Principal Love said.

I turned to my father. He would understand. "But, Dad, what I was trying to do—"

My father stood up. "Are you aware of the chaos you created, Hank? First of all, you didn't follow the rules. You can't just make up your own assignment."

"Yes, but I wanted to—"

"Don't interrupt your father," my mother said. I couldn't believe it. Even Mom was on their side. I thought maybe it was the shoes. She usually wears sandals, but she had put on her black leather loafers, the ones that look like Ms. Adolf's shoes. She's not as much fun when she wears those shoes.

"You were supposed to write an essay. Five paragraphs. That's with a pencil, Hank. Not papier-mâché." My father was seriously mad.

"But Dad, I remembered every fact I learned on our trip. I was writing it with my mouth. Like did you know that Niagara Falls is two thousand two hundred and twenty feet wide—and it's one hundred and seventy-three feet high and . . ."

"Enough of this," interrupted Principal Love. "We are here to decide on an appropriate punishment for what you've done."

At this moment I realized that the president

of the United States was not going to be inviting me to the White House.

"Detention for two weeks," Principal Love said.

"Grounded at home," my father added. "Same length of time."

My brain froze. Two weeks! The magic show—oh no! The magic show was right in the middle of my punishment.

I'm dead. I'm doomed. I'm out of the Magik 3.

CHAPTER 15

I LEFT PRINCIPAL LOVE'S office and headed downstairs to the lunchroom. A couple of first graders passed me on their way to the library.

"I think that's the boy who got in trouble," one of them whispered loudly. They stared at me like I had just robbed a bank or something. I spilled a little water on the floor. Big deal. Okay, a lot of water. Okay, a whole lot of water.

What does a guy do in this situation? I figured the only thing to do was wave. I went into my best Hank Zipzer strut.

"Good to see you," I said, grinning at them. "What's up in show-and-tell today?"

I think I scared them because they ran away. I continued downstairs. Some kids were already leaving the lunchroom and heading out to the yard. I passed Ryan and Gerald. Ryan held up his hand for a high five.

"You're a riot, man," he said.

"Truly," said Justin and Ricky, who were following behind.

"Your buddies are still eating lunch at your regular spot," Ryan said, pointing in the general direction of our table.

I went over to the table and slid in next to Ashley. She was in the middle of telling Frankie and Robert how she was going to spend her money from the magic show.

"I already have nine dollars saved," she was saying. "With the ten dollars we'll each earn, I'll have enough to get the dolphin, which will complete my crystal sea family."

"I'd hold off on that dolphin," I said.

"How bad was Principal Love?" Frankie asked. "Paint the picture, Zip."

"It was ugly," I answered. "I didn't get one word in. What I did get was two weeks of detention at school, and two weeks of being grounded at home."

"With or without TV?" asked Frankie.

"That is without any electronic device

98

known to mankind," I said.

Frankie grabbed his heart and fell to the ground. "Just the thought of it makes me stop breathing."

"Of course they're going to let you out for the magic show," Ashley said. She was twirling her ponytail in her fingers, which she does when she's worried.

"No," I answered. I didn't have the courage to look at her. "They said no exceptions."

"I can take his place," Robert chimed in.

"No, you can't," we answered together.

If what was happening wasn't bad enough, suddenly a dark cloud appeared. Its name was Nick McKelty.

"Oh, poor thing, did Principal Love bust you hard?" the big creep said in this stupid baby voice. His teeth were looking especially snaggly.

"Hank got two weeks detention," Robert volunteered. As you've probably already noticed, Robert doesn't know when to keep his mouth shut.

"What are you going to do about your grandpa's magic show at my dad's bowling alley?" Nick said. "Sounds like it's not happening." He was really enjoying this.

Before I had a chance to answer, he threw his big, slimy arm around me. He put his face up to mine, and there it was—the bad breath again. I didn't breathe.

"Hey don't worry about it, Zipper man," he said. "I got you covered."

"*You*?" I said, taking a breath and removing his arm from my shoulder. "What can *you* do, McKelty?"

"I'll put on a bowling show. I'll knock down more pins than . . . than . . . than . . ." I could see him searching for something clever to say, but as usual, he came up empty.

"I'll knock down a whole lot of pins," he finally spit out. "I just have to decide if I should use my left hand or my right hand."

"For your information," said Ashley, "the bowling league doesn't want to see *bowling*. They know how to do that. They want to see *magic*. That's why they hired us."

"My ball handling is magical," McKelty said. He was really happy with that comeback. He reached over and in one swipe with his apelike hand, nabbed Robert's Jell-O swirl and Ashley's Nestlé Crunch right off the table.

"Don't feel bad," he said as he walked away. "There's always next year."

We were silent. We didn't feel bad. We felt horrible.

"Hey, come on guys," I said with fake cheerfulness. "You can do the show without me!"

"We can't build the hat without you," said Ashley. "You're the one who knows how to do everything."

"Besides, who do you think is going to get Cheerio inside the hat?" asked Frankie. "Do you think that dog is going to listen to me? Not in this century."

I knew they were right. I had ruined everything for them.

I told them I was sorry.

But I don't think it helped.

CHAPTER 16

THE BELL RANG at three o'clock. Everyone grabbed their backpacks and headed for the door. They were on their way to soccer practice or sax lessons or other fun after-school activities. But not me. Nope. I was about to start my first day of detention. It was going to be me in a chair and Ms. Adolf at her desk for the next fun-filled hour.

I must have really sighed loudly.

"Do you have something to say?" Ms. Adolf asked.

I didn't say a word. I made a sound. The human body does that sometimes.

"Henry," Ms. Adolf said. "I assume you want to use this time wisely."

"Yes, Ms. Adolf," I answered. I couldn't imagine Ms. Adolf having a first name. Maybe her friends just call her Ms. Adolf.

"I've decided to have you write your composition under my supervision," she said. "Using paper and pencil, Henry. No monkey business this time."

I don't know why people always think monkey business is a bad thing. I love monkeys. They always seem to have such a good time, picking bugs off one another and eating them.

I took out a piece of paper and stared at it. It was blank. *So* blank. Ms. Adolf sat down at her desk and began to write in her brand new roll book. Neither one of us made a sound. It was so quiet, I could hear her breathing.

The clock on the wall clicked and the big hand jerked forward. One minute down, fifty-nine to go. Suddenly, the classroom door flew open and a messenger from the office came in. She handed Ms. Adolf a note and disappeared just as quickly. After Ms. Adolf read the note, she got her purse from the bottom drawer.

"I have an emergency that I have to deal with," she said. Her pet fire-breathing dragon must have gotten sick. "My husband's car won't start, and I have to pick him up from work."

Husband? Someone married her? No way.

Do you think he kisses her goodnight?

I must have wrinkled up my face, because Ms. Adolf said, "What's the face for, Henry?"

"Umm . . . I was just thinking about . . . umm . . . how it would feel for a raisin to try to lift up an elephant," I said.

"You would do better to keep your mind on your work, Henry, and not fill your head with silly thoughts." Ms. Adolf put the roll book in the top drawer and locked it with her shiny key. She scribbled a note on a Post-it, and gave it to me.

"The office has arranged for you to spend the rest of the hour in the music room with Mr. Rock, the music teacher. He's on his way. Go there and give him this note. Sit quietly until he arrives."

The music room is in the basement. Even though it's right next to the lunchroom, I don't go there unless I have to. Being there makes me remember my second-grade chorus tryouts, which I've been trying to forget ever since they happened. That was when Mrs. Peacock, the music teacher, told me that if I wanted to be in the chorus, I couldn't sing out loud. I was only allowed to mouth the words so I wouldn't throw everyone else off key. Mrs. Peacock left last year to have a baby. I had never met Mr. Rock. He was new.

The first things I noticed when I went in the music room were the posters all around the room. Most of them were of composers—Beethoven and Mozart and all those old guys. But there were other posters too—cool ones. Pink Floyd. A super-size photo of Manhattan from the air. An action shot of Michael Jordan going up for a tomahawk dunk. And my favorite, a picture of the coolest 1959 red-and-white Corvette you've ever seen.

A whole bunch of instruments were spread out in the room. There were triangles and xylophones and a piano. I sat down in a chair facing a set of silver-and-burgundy drums. I realized that my leg was bouncing up and down, about a mile a minute. It does that sometimes when I'm supposed to be sitting still.

As I sat there, it hit me that I had two whole weeks of misery in front of me. It didn't seem fair. I was being punished for trying to do my best.

Thoughts started coming from every corner of my brain. I wished Principal Love had let me finish just one sentence. I wished my parents had given me a chance to tell them how much I know about Niagara Falls. I wished I were as smart as my sister. She can do anything. She just toilet trained her parakeet. My parents are always so proud of her.

I picked up one of the drumsticks and tapped the big drum. It felt good. I liked the sound. I hit it again, a little louder. Then I picked up the other stick, and looked around to make sure I was still alone. *Bam!* I hit the drum, first with one stick, then the other. *Bam, bam, bam.* The drums were starting to sound like I felt.

Bam. I wish I didn't always forget my backpack.

Bam. I wish I could do long division.

Bam. I wish I didn't feel so stupid all the time.

Before I knew it, I was hitting the drums so fast I could hardly see my hands. The cymbal was right in front of me. Why not? I hit it. *Clash.* The sound vibrated all around the room.

I smacked it again. Now back to the drums. *Bam, clash, boom!*

"That's for detention!" I shouted.

Clash, boom, bam!

"That's for always getting into trouble!" My voice rang out.

Bam, bam, bammitty bam!

"That's five, one for each paragraph I can't write!"

Bam, boom, bam, boom, bam, boom, boom!

"And that's for my stupid brain!" I yelled.

From behind me, I heard a man's voice say, "I'll bet your brain isn't stupid."

I froze, then slowly turned around. The man in the doorway had a young face but a head full of curly, silver hair. He was wearing a blue denim shirt and a tie with musical notes on it.

"Mr. Rock?" I asked.

"That's me," he answered. "Does your band have a CD out yet?"

"I'm really sorry," I said. "I know I wasn't supposed to touch these, but—"

"They're instruments," Mr. Rock said. "They're here to play. Sounds like they helped you express yourself."

107

"I had a bad day," I said.

"Because of your stupid brain?" he asked.

"Yeah. How did you know?"

"Because you just said it," he said with a smile. "It was hard to miss."

I handed Mr. Rock the note from Ms. Adolf. He read it, then pulled up a chair and sat down backward on it. I assumed he was going to ask me why I was on detention, but he didn't.

"So, your name is Henry Zipzer?" he said.

"My friends call me Hank."

"Hank, that's a good name," he said. "Ever heard of Hank Aaron?"

"April eighth, 1974," I answered. "The day Hammerin' Hank beat Babe Ruth's home-run record."

"I'm a baseball fan, too," he said. "I don't suppose you know what number home run Hank Aaron hit on that day."

"Seven hundred fifteen. Do you want to know a weird Hank Aaron fact?"

"Sure," said Mr. Rock.

"In four of his twenty-three seasons in base-ball, Hank Aaron hit exactly forty-four homeruns, which was his uniform number.

Pretty amazing, huh?"

"Seems to me," said Mr. Rock, "that your brain isn't as stupid as you think. It's got plenty of good information tucked inside it."

"I don't have a problem remembering interesting facts," I explained. "I just can't do a lot with them. Like writing essays and spelling are tough—stuff that's easy for everyone else."

"Everybody learns differently," he said. "*Your* brain is *your* brain. You just have to figure out the right way to feed it."

"I gave it a lot of Cocoa Puffs this morning," I said.

"How about music?" he laughed. "Do you ever feed it music?"

He actually waited for an answer.

"No," I said.

Mr. Rock rubbed his hands together as though he was about to eat something delicious.

"I'll make a deal with you," he said. "Ms. Adolf's note says you're supposed to work on your essay. We've got forty-five minutes of detention left. Let's take a few minutes and listen to some music. It might put you in the writing mood. What do you like?"

"Well, my essay is supposed to be about Niagara Falls."

"Let me see if I can find some water music," he said. "What does Niagara Falls sound like?"

"It sounded like thunder when I was there."

He shuffled through some CDs and picked one out.

"This is part of the Grand Canyon Suite," he said. "It's called *Cloud Burst*." He put it on, then turned it up loud. It really felt as though it were raining right there in the basement of PS 87. I'm not kidding.

Papa Pete says that you never know where good luck is going to come from. In my case, it came from Big Harry's Auto and Body Shop, which took the entire week to fix Mr. Adolf's car. Ms. Adolf had to leave early every day to pick up her husband, so I got to spend one whole week of detention with Mr. Rock.

He taught me how to play "Hey Jude" on the xylophone. We looked at magazine pictures of our favorite cars. I picked the Ferrari F-50 convertible, and he picked a 1947 Ford woody with a surfboard on top. He put me in total charge of trimming the dead leaves off his indoor plants. I liked that job.

We worked on my essay, too. When I got stuck, which was every other second of every other minute, he'd ask me questions like "How did the falls make you feel?" or "What did you like best about the trip?" That really helped me focus.

The best part was when we listened to music. He'd put on a CD and then we'd just sit back and let music fill the room.

It felt so good, I couldn't believe I was in school.

CHAPTER 17
Grounded

"WHAT'S A NINE-LETTER French word for eggplant?" my father shouted to no one in particular.

I was sitting at the other end of the dining room table, doodling in my math workbook. As part of my punishment, my parents took away my privacy privileges. I wasn't allowed to do my homework in my bedroom. The worst part was having to listen to my father's crossword puzzle questions. I don't get it. What's the point of doing crossword puzzles if you have to ask everyone else for the answers?

Emily walked out of her bedroom with Katherine on her shoulder. Her long tongue was darting in and out of her mouth—Katherine's tongue, that is, not Emily's.

"Has anyone seen Katherine's bag of dinner pellets?" Emily asked.

"I put them in the cookie jar, honey," Mom called from the kitchen.

"Mom!" I yelled. "I ate those for my snack this afternoon. I thought they were one of your new healthy treats."

Emily laughed. Katherine jiggled up and down on her shoulder.

"It's not funny," I said. "Now I'll probably grow a long, disgusting iguana tongue."

As I was rinsing my mouth out at the kitchen sink, the doorbell rang.

"I'll get it," I yelled.

"Remember to look through the peephole first," Mom reminded me.

If I stand on my toes, I can just barely get my eye up to the peephole. I looked out but didn't see anyone.

"Who is it?" I shouted through the door.

"It's us," Frankie whispered. "Open up, Zip."

I pressed my face up against the crack in the door. "I'm grounded," I whispered back. "You know I can't play."

"We're not here to see you," Frankie said. "We're here to talk to your dad."

I opened the door. Frankie and Ashley marched right by me, with Robert bringing up the rear.

"Good evening, Mr. Z," Frankie said, going right up to my father.

"We've come to discuss a very important business matter," added Ashley.

My father looked up from his crossword puzzle.

"You kids aren't supposed to be here," he said. "Hank is still grounded for another week."

"This matter can't wait," said Ashley.

"Aubergine," said Robert, looking at the newspaper in my father's hand.

"What's that supposed to mean?" snapped Frankie.

"It means eggplant in French," said Robert, pointing to the blank spaces on my father's crossword puzzle. "Thirteen across is *aubergine*."

"Sometimes you scare me," Frankie said to Robert.

"Come on, boys, let's not forget why we're here," Ashley said. She turned to my father, with her no-nonsense face on. "Mr. Zipzer, as you know, Magik 3 has a contract with Papa Pete to put on a fantastical magic show this weekend at McKelty's Roll 'N Bowl. We've tried all week to build the special hat we need for the grand finale. But our hat looks like a couch."

"We're begging you, Mr. Z.," said Frankie. "We're *pleading* with you. Free Hank. We can't build the hat without him."

My father shook his head no.

"I'll help you with forty-three down," Robert offered. "Oh, I also happen to know three across."

"I'm afraid Hank has to learn his lesson," my father interrupted. "There'll be other magic shows."

He stood up, went to the front door, and held it open. You couldn't get a much more final "no" than that. Frankie, Ashley, and Robert left. My father closed the door and started back to his chair. The doorbell rang again. My father spun around and yanked the door open.

"Now listen, kids," he began. Then he

115

stopped suddenly. The next thing I heard was him saying, "I'm sorry, can I help you?"

I got up to see who was at the front door.

What is Mr. Rock doing here? Oh no. I bet I broke the drum and he's here to tell my parents. I hit myself on the forehead with my fist. Not hard, but like I do sometimes when I'm frustrated with myself. How could I have been so stupid?

"I hope I'm not interrupting your dinner," Mr. Rock said. "I'm Donald Rock, the music teacher from PS 87. I was wondering if I could talk with you for a moment?"

My father opened the door wider and led Mr. Rock into the living room.

I was surprised to see him. I had never had a teacher pop in before. But then again, Mr. Rock wasn't like other teachers.

"What's he doing here?" Emily whispered to me. "You must have messed up big-time."

My mother came out of the kitchen, drying her hands on a green checkered dish towel. She picked up a plate from the dining room table and offered Mr. Rock a cracker with some of her new soy cheddar cheese spread. He popped it into his mouth before I had a chance to warn him. His lips stuck together when he tried to talk.

"I had the pleasure of spending last week with your son during his detention," Mr. Rock began. He scraped some of the soy cheese spread off the roof of his mouth, trying to smile at the same time. My mother offered him another cracker but, smart guy that he is, Mr. Rock said no thanks.

"I've had a lot of time to talk with Hank and to observe him. I've noticed that he is somewhat frustrated about his schoolwork," he said.

"Very frustrated," my mother added.

"Mr. and Mrs. Zipzer, I believe Hank might benefit from being tested—to see if he has any learning differences." Mr. Rock waited for their answer.

"There's nothing wrong with Hank," my father said. "If he spent as much time doing his schoolwork as he does daydreaming and puttering around his room and building things, he'd be an A student. Hank is just lazy."

"Maybe that's not the case," Mr. Rock said. "You know, many children have learning challenges. Every child's brain is wired differently."

Every brain is wired differently? What was he saying? That my brain is messed up? Oh that's great. Now everyone will really think I'm stupid!

"What does that mean, 'wired differently'?" my mom asked.

"Different kids learn in different ways," Mr. Rock said. "I know that because I myself had difficulty in school."

"Hank's sister, Emily, is an excellent student," my father said. "She doesn't seem to have any school problems."

Emily held an iguana pellet in the palm of her hand. Katherine whipped out her long tongue and snapped it up. I'll tell you one thing—Emily may not have school problems, but she has weird taste in pets.

"I'm sure you're very proud of Emily," Mr. Rock continued, "but having a sister who excels adds to the pressure on Hank."

"What pressure?" said my father. "Hank doesn't worry about anything. *That's* his problem."

My mother was studying me very carefully. My leg was bouncing up and down again. She was watching it.

"Stan, can we at least talk about this?" she asked.

"I think that's a good idea," Mr. Rock said. "You have a lot to think about. I just thought it was better to have this conversation in person rather than on the phone. Give me a call if you want to talk further."

Mr. Rock turned to me.

"Hank, we've been talking *about* you but not *to* you. Do you have any questions?"

"Just one," I said. "Let's say a person in the fourth grade might have learning challenges. And that person wanted to do something that was very creative, like for example a magic show, which included earning, let's say, a ten-dollar bill. Don't you think that person should be allowed to do it because he tries so hard at everything?"

"I think creativity should always be encouraged." Mr. Rock smiled.

He stood up to go. He shook hands with everybody, including Katherine. She must have liked him too, because her tongue shot out and gave his hand a sticky lick.

As soon as Mr. Rock was gone, I turned to my parents.

"You wouldn't go against the advice of a teacher, would you?" I asked. I had great hope in my heart. "Please . . . can I just do the magic show?"

My mother and father looked at each other for what seemed like a year and a half.

"We'll get back to you on this," my father finally answered.

CHAPTER 18

THEY GOT BACK to me the next morning.
They said yes.

The show was on!

Magik 3 was back in business. I was so excited that if you hold this book to your ear, you can hear me jumping up and down.

CHAPTER 19

AT EXACTLY SEVEN O'CLOCK Saturday night, we pushed the giant hat through the swinging doors of McKelty's Roll 'N Bowl. If I do say so myself, the hat was awesome. It was big and black and it had wheels. We even built the secret pocket inside, where Cheerio could hide until it was time to pull him out. To keep him happy, we put doggie treats inside the pocket with him.

McKelty's was jammed with people. It was opening night for bowling league season. There were twelve teams. Each had their own lane and their own shirts. Papa Pete and The Chopped Livers were on Lane Five, warming up. In the middle of the bowling alley, where they usually serve pizza at birthday parties, my mom had put out sandwiches. Papa Pete had warned her that anything with soy was out of the question. It had to be the real thing. I could smell the hot pastrami on fresh rye. My mouth started to water, but I knew we had more important things to do before we ate.

"Attention bowlers," came a voice from the loudspeaker. I knew that voice.

"Magik 3 couldn't be with us tonight because one of its members was grounded for being too stupid to write his essay," the voice said.

The McKelty Factor strikes again.

"Instead we have something much better— a thrilling, unbelievably death-defying bowling exhibition that stars me."

Leave it to Nick McKelty to put together a show starring only himself.

"That slimy toad thinks he's taking our spot," Ashley said.

"Yeah, well, I hope that slimy toad can swim because I'm going to flush him down the toilet," Frankie growled.

The loudspeaker crackled again. "For my first feat, I'm going to bowl a strike with my left hand. Blindfolded."

Before we knew it, Nick appeared on lane

ten. The jerk was actually wearing a blindfold. Everyone watched as he brought the ball up to his chest. On his bowling ball was a big picture of his slimy face. Unbelievable!

He took one, two, three steps toward the line and let the ball fly off his fingers. It landed on the lane with a *thud* and rolled smack into the gutter. The crowd moaned. I knew this was our opportunity.

I jumped up onto one of the benches and said, "Ladies and gentlemen, how about that Nick McKelty, the bowling whiz. Doesn't he look great in a blindfold? Let's give it up for him."

Everyone laughed. I motioned for Frankie and Robert to wheel out the hat.

Nick looked stunned. He tried to take off his blindfold, but he had tied the knot too tightly.

"While we're setting up for the real entertainment, take a moment to enjoy the mouth acrobatics of Miss Ashley Wong, as she tries to tie not one, but two cherry stems into a knot, never once using her hands," I said with pride.

I handed Ashley two cherries from the bar. She popped them into her mouth, scrunching up her face and moving her tongue a mile a minute. As she worked, she strolled around the audience, showing off her T-shirt with the red rhinestone cherries. By the time she got back to where she began, she had produced two knotted cherry stems, connected at the top. They looked like a small Christmas tree. Papa Pete led the applause.

Frankie gave me the nod. He was ready to go.

"Now, ladies and gentlemen, for the main event, I'm happy to present the freestyling magic of Frankie Townsend and Magik 3," I announced.

"Hey, what about my bowling tricks?" Nick McKelty shouted. He had finally managed to untie his blindfold. His eyes looked blazing mad. "I'm not done yet."

"Yes, you are," the crowd yelled back.

Nick ran into his father's office to sulk.

Frankie moved right into his act. He pulled scarves from his sleeve, cut a rope into three pieces and put it back together, and pushed a pencil through the center of a quarter that he borrowed from Papa Pete. That truly is one of my favorite tricks. And Frankie, that rat, won't tell me how he does it.

Ashley and Robert wheeled out the hat while I kept watch on Cheerio, trying to keep him calm. He was getting that look in his eye, his pre-spinning look.

"Not now, Cheerio," I whispered to him, scratching him between the ears. He loves that. "Don't go crazy on me, boy."

"And now, for my grand finale," announced Frankie. "At the special request of Papa Pete, I will pull a small, live, furry thing from this magical top hat!"

"It's probably a stuffed teddy bear," McKelty shouted from the office doorway. "I'm sure everyone would rather see me throw a strike backward, between my legs, again using my left hand. Wouldn't you?"

It was his father who gave him the answer everyone else was thinking.

"Be quiet, Nick," he said, "and enjoy the show."

"Here we have a hat," Frankie began, point-ing to our giant top hat. "My assistants will show you the inside of the hat." Ashley and I tipped the hat forward so everyone could see in. Cheerio was tucked in his secret pocket so you couldn't see him. I thought I heard a tiny yip as he slid against the side.

"Notice that it's actually empty," Robert said with this kind of goofy smile. We had decided to give him a line.

"I will now take my cape and cover the hat," Frankie said. He showed the audience both sides of the cape, and laid it over the hat like a tablecloth. The place was silent, except if you stood close enough to the hat, you could hear the crunch, crunch, crunch of doggie treats inside Cheerio's mouth.

"Hank, the magic words, if you please," Frankie said.

I stepped forward, closed my eyes, and waved my hands over the cape. We hadn't rehearsed that part, but I thought it added a lot to the moment. I chanted:

"Something live, something furry,
appear now, in a hurry."

"*Zengawii!*" Frankie shouted, as he pulled

the cape off of the hat. People in the audience moved to the edge of their seats. Everyone was completely quiet. Frankie reached into the hat. Suddenly there was a sound! It was the growl of one very angry little dog. Frankie pulled his hand out of the hat really fast. Cheerio stuck his face out, his paws hanging over the brim of the hat. He looked at the audience. I don't think he'd ever seen so many people in one place.

The audience burst into laughter and applause, which must have really scared Cheerio, because he dove back into the bottom of the hat and started to spin. And I don't mean just regular spinning. No, this was mega-spinning. He was going so fast that the hat started to move down a lane.

"Is this part of the trick?" I whispered to Frankie.

"He's your dog, Zip. Don't ask me," he answered.

By that time, the hat was rocketing down the lane. It turned around and around, picking up speed from the oil on the wood. In no time, it was at the end of the lane. *Smack!* The hat crashed into the pins, sending them flying in every direction. Nine pins went down. The last one teetered back and forth, back and forth. Almost . . . yes . . . no . . . yes . . . finally, it fell.

The crowd gasped.

"How about that for a strike!" Papa Pete yelled.

The place went wild. Everyone was applauding—everyone but Nick McKelty. He just stood by the sandwiches, scowling.

"Hey, doesn't anyone want to see my world-famous left-handed trick shot?" he yelled.

"Give it up, Nick!" I said to him. "You can't top the hat!"

He was so mad, his face turned bright red.

"Fine," he said. "Then I'm getting a Vanilla Coke. And you can't have one!"

"Is he the comeback king or what?" Ashley said. We all laughed as he stomped off.

Cheerio was out of the hat by now, sliding down the lane as he tried to make his way toward me. He looked like he was on ice skates. I think he was still feeling dizzy, because his eyes were spinning in opposite directions. I scooped him up and gave him a big hug.

I turned around. All the people in the

bowling alley were on their feet cheering—for Cheerio and for us, the Magik 3.

Frankie, Ashley, Robert, and I joined hands and took a bow. It was the greatest feeling of my entire life.

CHAPTER 20

THERE'S A LITTLE BALCONY off our living room. It's my favorite place because at night you can see the moon from there. As I sat on the balcony and looked up at the moon, I thought about how great it feels to actually do something right.

Papa Pete slid the door open and brought out two pickles—my favorite bedtime snack. Mine was an old dill, and his was a crunchy garlic. He sat down next to me and said, "You should be very proud tonight, Hank."

"I really am," I said.

We were quiet for a while, just sitting there, enjoying our pickles.

"They want to test me," I said finally

"In what, math?" Papa Pete asked.

"A teacher came over to our house. He said

I might have learning challenges. He said my brain might be different."

"We're all different," said Papa Pete. "That's what makes us great."

"But what if the test shows that I'm stupid?"

"Grandson of mine, there is nothing stupid about you. Didn't you build that project for school? Didn't you figure out how to make the hat work? Didn't you amaze every one of my friends tonight at the bowling alley? You're a winner, Hank."

"But I'm different."

"Take pickles," said Papa Pete. "There are big ones and little ones, smooth ones and bumpy ones, very crunchy ones and not-so-crunchy ones. There are bread-and-butter pickles, gherkins, hamburger slices, half-dills, full-dills . . ."

"Okay, Papa Pete, I get the picture."

"The point is this," he said. "They're all different and they're all delicious to someone. And you, my grandson, are positively delicious."

I looked down at the little bit of pickle I had

left. I popped it into my mouth. It was really good.

Then I looked at Papa Pete. He really knows a lot about everything. I sure hope he's right about me!

About the Authors

HENRY WINKLER is an actor, producer, and director and he speaks publicly all over the world. Holy mackerel! No wonder he needs a nap. He lives in Los Angeles with his wife, Stacey. They have three children named Jed, Zoe, and Max and two dogs named Monty and Charlotte. If you gave him one word to describe how he feels about this book, he would say, "Proud."

If you gave him two words, he would say, "I am so happy that I got a chance to write this book with Lin and I really hope you enjoy it." That's twenty-two words, but hey, he's got learning challenges.

LIN OLIVER is a writer and producer of movies, books and television series for children and families. She has created over one hundred episodes of television, four movies and seven books. She lives in Los Angeles with her husband, Alan. They have three sons named Theo, Ollie, and Cole, one fluffy dog named Annie, and no iguanas.

If you gave her two words to describe this book, she would say "funny" and "compassionate." If you asked her what compassionate meant, she would say "full of kindness." She would not make you look it up in the dictionary.